The STRANGER

ANNE SCHRAFF

A Boy Called Twister

Dark Secrets

Deliverance

The Fairest

If You Really Loved Me

Leap of Faith

Like a Broken Doll

The Lost

No Fear

One of Us

Outrunning the Darkness

The Quality of Mercy

Shadows of Guilt

The Stranger

Time of Courage

To Be a Man

To Catch a Dream

The Unforgiven

The Water's Edge

Wildflower

ISBN-13: 978-1-61651-266-8
ISBN-10: 1-61651-266-0
eBook: 978-1-60291-991-4

Printed in Guangzhou, China
1010/10-25-10

16 15 14 13 12   1 2 3 4 5

CHAPTER ONE

Ernesto Sandoval passed his aunt's restaurant every morning on his way to Cesar Chavez High School, where he was beginning his junior year. *Tía* Hortencia's homemade tamales were the toast of the *barrio*. Everybody knew that Hortencia made the best tamales in the world. Ernesto's one and only friend at his new school, Abel Ruiz, said, "She must make a fortune in there. There's always a crowd of people wanting to get in."

Ernesto's extended family had lived in this *barrio* for generations. But Ernesto, his parents, and his two sisters had been living in Los Angeles for ten years. They'd just moved back. Luis Sandoval, Ernesto's father, taught history at a high school in Los Angeles. He was laid off because of budget cuts. When he got the offer to teach at Chavez, he jumped at the chance. Ernesto remembered many nights when his parents would be up late in Los Angeles. They'd be talking about finances and what to do if Luis couldn't find another job. "My sister Hortencia joked with me," Dad said one night. "She said if all else fails, I can work with her at the restaurant making tamales, preparing the *masa* to put the filling in." Dad had laughed nervously at that prospect. He loved teaching. It was his life.

Ernesto also loved his high school in Los Angeles. He had friends there he'd known since first grade. He had a nice girlfriend, Gabriella. The relationship was not serious, but she was fun to hang out with. Ernesto had felt comfortable in the LA high school. He had not lived here since he was six years old.

There were a lot of cliques at Chavez High. Each clique seemed impenetrable to outsiders. A stranger like Ernesto was not welcome inside them. Ernesto had played some baseball in middle school, but he wasn't a jock. The only sport he really liked was running. But, even so, he had been turned down when he tried to join the track team in LA.

"You used to live around here when you were a little kid, huh Ernie?" Abel asked as they walked together to school.

"Yeah," Ernesto replied ruefully. "I was six when we moved. Dad was still in college. My mom worked in a haircutting store to pay the bills. Then Dad graduated and got this teaching job at a high school in Los Angeles. So we moved there. It was great. Dad loved his job, and Mom was able to quit working and stay home. My little sisters were born up there. Now Dad is trying to fit in teaching at Chavez. He's a stranger too, like me."

Ernesto was grateful that he didn't have any classes that Dad taught. He figured having his father as the teacher would be awkward. Luis Sandoval was a tall, thin, dark-skinned man, very handsome and dignified looking. He was much darker than Mom. Mom told Ernesto once that her own grandmother had laughed and said Mom's fiancé was *Indio*. "*Indio*" was a prejudiced word. Mom told Ernesto she didn't care about that. She fell madly in love with Dad when they were only teenagers.

Ernesto worried that maybe his serious father would not fit in at Chavez High anymore than he, Ernesto, was fitting in. Luis Sandoval did not make jokes and banter with his students, as some of the other teachers did. Ernesto worried that the kids wouldn't like him and that maybe he wouldn't be asked back next year. The move from LA had been expensive. A lot of bills had piled up.

The boys passed a high fence covered with graffiti and some graphic art too. The art looked pretty good to Ernesto. The fence had a fire-breathing dragon and a fierce-looking eagle reaching out with its talons.

"Dudes who drop out of Chavez come around here at night and decorate the fences and the walls of buildings," Abel explained. "We got a lotta kids dropping outta Chavez. It's a big problem. Teachers always griping about it. Sometimes they're just taggers, but lotta them join gangs too." Abel shrugged. "What're you gonna do?"

As they neared the school, Ernesto glanced at the stream of students. Maybe ten years ago he played with some of them, but he didn't remember. What does a six-year-old kid remember? Most of the students were texting or talking on their phones. They were in a world of their own. They didn't even seem to notice the people around them. Ernesto had a phone too, but whom was he going to text? Abel, his only friend, who was walking beside him?

Ernesto felt invisible as he drew closer to the school. The buildings looked cold and block-like—like blocks of ice. The only appealing feature was a mural out front bearing the kindly face of Cesar Chavez. In the mural, Chavez was standing in a field surrounded by weary-looking farm workers. Ernesto remembered reading a short biography of Chavez. He was a good man who spent his short life helping farm workers earn a living wage. He died, probably of exhaustion, when he was sixty-six.

Yesterday Ernesto noticed a really pretty girl in his English class. She was wearing a pink sweater and jeans that fit awfully good. Seeing her was the only good thing that happened in English class. Ernesto could hardly keep his eyes off her. She looked up from texting once before class began, and Ernesto tried to smile at her. But he was so nervous that his smile came off as a grimace, and the girl looked away. He didn't blame her.

Now as Ernesto and Abel walked into English class and took their seats, Ernesto looked for her again. There she was, this time in a bright red T-shirt. Abel saw Ernesto staring at her, and he said, "That's one hot chili pepper, eh man?"

"Yeah!" Ernesto agreed. "You know her?" For a minute, Ernesto thought she might be Abel's girl. He sure didn't want to tick off the only friend he had at Chavez.

"That's Naomi Martinez," Abel replied. "I know her to say 'hi' to her, but I don't mess with her. She's got a boyfriend, and he's real possessive. She's a cheerleader and he's a jock. It's the same old story, man."

Ernesto decided he wouldn't smile at her anymore.

"Her boyfriend plays for the Chavez Cougars," Abel went on. "Pretty good linebacker and good-looking, but stupid. Hanging on to a C in most classes and worrying about losing his eligibility to play. Clay Aguirre. First-class creep."

Ernesto thought back fondly to his school in Los Angeles and Gabriella. She was easy to be with. She and Ernesto had nothing heavy going, just holding hands sometimes and a few pecks on the lips. Ernesto wondered whether there was anybody like Gabriella around at Chavez High.

The English teacher, Ms. Hunt, came in. She was an Anglo, young and cool and sort of pretty. She made some lame jokes about how excited everybody must be about studying good old Shakespeare. Most of the students were Latino, but there were a few Asians, African Americans, and Filipinos, along with some Anglos. Ernesto could see that the kids liked Ms. Hunt. He hoped that the kids in American History I were liking his dad as much. He wouldn't be making jokes, though. He'd be teaching very seriously about the explorers coming to the New World. Luis Sandoval was a serious man. He was kind and dedicated but not out to win a popularity contest.

Ernesto's father graduated from California State at Northridge. He graduated *magna cum laude,* and then he got his master's degree. Ernesto was only seven when he watched Dad get his master's. Luis Sandoval was the first in his family to graduate from college, and graduating with honors was awesome. Ernesto remembered the day, watching his father marching in the solemn procession of scholars. Ernesto's grandparents, *Abuela* Lena and *Abuelo* Luis Senior, wept tears of joy as their boy's name was called out. Ernesto remembered his grandmother turning to him, squeezing his arm, and whispering, "*Mi hijo! Mi hijo! Su padre!*"

Now, Ernesto was thinking, Luis Sandoval was standing before a class of teenagers here at Chavez High School. Maybe they didn't like the serious, dignified man who didn't crack jokes. Maybe word of their dissatisfaction would reach the administration office. Maybe the administration would think that this new teacher, who had lost his job in Los Angeles, was not very good. Maybe they would tell him that he should move on. The thought sent a shudder through Ernesto's body, not only because the family was in a shaky financial situation and his Dad needed the job. More important,

Ernesto loved his Dad, and the thought that his proud father would be so humiliated hurt him. Ernesto felt sorry for his father. He felt sorry for himself too.

"We're starting with something fun," Ms. Hunt chortled. "A lovely story of a bloody impending murder!"

Everybody laughed. Ms. Hunt asked, "What is the story of *Macbeth* about?"

Naomi Martinez raised her hand. When Ms. Hunt nodded toward her, she answered, "It's about Lady Macbeth and how she pushes her husband to do violence."

"Exactly," Ms. Hunt said. "Let's face it. Isn't that just the sort of story we love? Look at what we watch on television. Stories about murders, detectives, plotting. If there's not at least one dead body on the screen, we feel cheated. When those gory images appear, don't we widen our eyes a little bit?"

Everyone laughed again. "How do we find out right away that horrible events are coming?" Ms. Hunt asked.

A handsome boy replied, "The witches are there cackling about fair is foul and saying stuff about the fog and filthy air."

Abel nudged Ernesto and whispered, "Clay Aguirre."

Ernesto looked more closely at the boy. He had thick, blue-black hair and perfect features. He was built too. Ernesto figured Clay was way better-looking than he was. Mom told Ernesto all the time how handsome he was, but Ernesto figured that was bull. He was too skinny for one thing, only about a hundred and fifty pounds on a frame reaching over six feet now. Aguirre looked like he was about one-eighty at least.

"Right, Clay," Ms. Hunt responded. "That is a portent of things to come." She smiled at Clay. She probably liked him. She was thirty-something, young enough to notice a good-looking guy, but much too professional to go over that firm line between teacher and student.

Clay enjoyed the teacher's approval. He glanced over at Naomi, expecting that she had noticed his moment in the sun. But Naomi's smile was only an afterthought, and Clay looked annoyed. Clearly he expected her to focus on him every minute.

"What a jerk," Ernesto thought to himself.

"Ernesto," Ms. Hunt said, "would you read the first quote of scene two and tell us what it means to you?"

Ernesto looked down at his open book. He hated speaking out in class. "Uh, it says—uh, *he* says," Ernesto began.

"*Who* says, Ernesto?" Ms. Hunt asked. Her tone was sympathetic. She seemed like a nice lady, but she probably thought Ernesto was stupid. He wasn't. He made excellent grades in his high school in Los Angeles. He even aced the hard science and math classes.

"Uh, the king, Duncan," Ernesto replied. His voice cracked a little. A few students seemed about to laugh, but Ms. Hunt discouraged them with a stern look. She was good—cool but able to control a class.

"King Duncan," Ernesto continued, "he asks 'what bloody man is that?' And they're talking about a revolt."

"Right," Ms. Hunt affirmed, smiling at Ernesto. She seemed glad he'd pulled it off.

"She probably thinks I'm some pathetic loser," Ernesto thought. "And she wants to encourage me."

The class continued, and Ernesto had to admit Ms. Hunt made it interesting. She was a better teacher than his English teacher in LA. Ernesto liked Ms. Hunt. He figured he would do okay in her class. When the bell rang, everybody left the classroom in an orderly fashion. Ernesto had been in a few classrooms where the ringing of the bell launched a stampede for the door. As Naomi Martinez was walking out, some papers fluttered from her binder to the floor. Since her papers landed at Ernesto's feet, he stooped to pick them up and handed them to her.

"Thanks," Naomi said with a bright smile. She wore cherry-red lipstick that stood out gloriously against her lovely mocha skin.

Clay Aguirre was right there, giving Ernesto a look that sent a chill through him. "Who're you, punk?" he demanded.

"Clay," Naomi said softly, "he just picked up my papers. They slipped from my binder and—"

"Just so you know, punk," Clay went on, stabbing a finger into Ernesto's chest, "she's taken. Okay?"

Ernesto stared at the guy. He was handsome, but right now his features were hard and ugly. Ernesto was amazed that a beautiful girl like Naomi found him appealing.

Clay put his arm around Naomi's shoulders. Then they walked out of the classroom together and into the flow of students. When they were out of earshot, Abel said, "You see what I mean, man?"

Ernesto nodded. "What's she need somebody like that for?" he mused.

"Chicks," Abel asserted. "Go figure. They go for the bad boys every time."

Ernesto looked at Abel. He was a tall, skinny kid too, like Ernesto. He had the added problem of a bad complexion. Ernie thought he had problems getting girls too, but maybe even worse. That common problem was why they bonded that first day. Maybe, Ernesto thought gloomily, they were two losers who found each other.

Ernesto's father had told him often that, as a young man, he too was dateless most of the time. He remained that way until his senior year in high school. He was on the dean's list, and he was a favorite of all the teachers. But his social life was dismal. Luis Sandoval was tall and skinny, like Ernesto. He also wore glasses. He was serious and quiet, and the girls acted as though he was a piece of the school furniture.

Then there was a talent show. Luis entered it because he had spotted a beautiful girl named Maria Vasquez. She had cascading reddish brown hair and a sweet personality. Luis didn't think he had a chance with such a girl, but he needed to be close to her, to try at least to gain her attention.

At the audition, Luis Sandoval sang a song from *Oklahoma*, and Maria Vasquez sang a song from *The Sound of Music*. They were both so good that they were paired in a duet that brought down the house. For the first time in the history of the school, *two* students won the talent show: Luis and Maria. They began dating and fell in love quickly. Ernesto's father always said he fell in love first, but his mother insisted she loved Luis before he loved her. They were married seventeen years ago, when they were both barely twenty. Even all these years later, Ernesto thought his mother was still one of the most beautiful women he had ever seen.

"Don't worry Ernesto," Dad said consolingly, "there is a special girl for you too. Some boys have a lot of girlfriends, but they don't mean anything. They are shallow. It's all about having fun, and the heart is not involved. Your mother and I, we knew we were right for each other. When the time comes, you will know too."

CHAPTER ONE

Ernesto texted Gabriella.

"How RU? I don't like it here. MUSM."

Gabriella texted back. "Hang in there. MU2."

Ernesto figured Gabriella was doing a lot better than he was. She still had all her friends. Gabriella was cute. She probably had another boyfriend already. Some other dude had taken Ernesto's place. But Ernesto was a stranger in town. Except for Abel, he didn't know anybody.

Ernesto spotted his father walking across the campus of Cesar Chavez High. His shoulders seemed to be slumping. Maybe his students had given him a hard time. Ernesto started worrying again. Poor Dad! Maybe Chavez High was as unwelcoming to Dad as it was to Ernesto. Maybe they were both treading water.

Ernesto's parents wanted four children when they were first married, two boys and two girls. They had a boy right away. Then, for eight years, no more came. Mom badly wanted another child. She had grown up an only child, and she had been lonely. Mom prayed and lit candles in church. Mom's parents said having just one child was maybe just as well. They didn't think much of Dad's prospects as a provider. Teachers were not well paid. But *Abuela* Lena Sandoval understood. Ernesto's father's mother prayed, said rosaries, and made novenas. She was sure her prayers would be answered. "There will be more *niños*," she foretold.

Then, when Ernesto was eight years old, Katalina arrived, a beautiful baby girl. Ernesto remembered the great joy in the Sandoval household. He remembered the explosion of pink balloons, pink blankets, even a pink teddy bear. Katalina was now a bright, bubbly eight-year-old. Then, two years later, came Juanita, who was more quiet and lovely. She was now six. Ernesto's father worried about providing for his wife and three children. He didn't want Ernesto's mother to work. She also wanted to stay home with her children, to greet them when they came home from school.

But Luis Sandoval worried. And sometimes Mom gently suggested that, now that the girls were now in school, she should work part-time. But Dad always smiled and said, "Maybe, if it comes to that, but not yet . . . not yet . . ."

Ernesto hoped Mom would not have to work. Not that Mom's working would be such a terrible thing, but Dad's pride would be hurt.

As Ernesto walked to his next class, he looked at the stream of students around him. They all looked like strange aliens from a very distant planet. They looked weird even though they dressed just like Ernesto did, in T-shirts and jeans. And they looked mean. He knew that they couldn't all be mean, but that's how they looked to him. Some of them were laughing. Ernesto felt as though they were laughing at him, but, of course, they weren't.

Ernesto did not feel like he belonged at Chavez High. He looked around desperately for Abel Ruiz. He needed to find Abel. Abel was like a lifeline reaching out to him. Ernesto felt as though he was drowning in an angry, dark, swirling sea. As long as Abel was near, he could cling to his hand. He'd be okay.

Ernesto wondered whether his father felt as he did right now—like a stranger in a strange land where the people didn't like him very much. He wondered if his father was afraid too.

CHAPTER TWO

"Hi," someone said to Ernesto. The voice was as soft as satin and girlish.

Ernesto turned to see Naomi Martinez. He was shocked.

"I just wanted to apologize to you for how Clay acted," she explained. "You were nice enough to pick up my stuff, and he was a jerk. He's not really like that. I'm sorry. I need to apologize."

Ernesto stared at the girl. "That's okay," he mumbled. How could such a nice girl like Clay Aguirre? Why was she apologizing for what that jerk did? Why was she lying and saying he wasn't really like that? Of course he was.

"You're new here at Chavez, aren't you?" Naomi asked. "I haven't seen you except in the last few days."

"Yeah," Ernesto replied, "we just moved down here from LA. My dad, he's uh . . . a history teacher here at school." He looked around nervously. He expected Clay Aguirre to spring from the oleander bushes along the sidewalk and lunge at him.

"Oh yeah?" Naomi responded. "What's your name?"

"Ernesto Sandoval," he responded. "My father is Luis Sandoval. He uh . . . teaches American History I and some world history."

"Oh wow, I have his class second period," Naomi exclaimed. "He's an excellent teacher. When I saw how young he was, I thought maybe he wouldn't know his stuff. But he's amazing."

Ernesto felt a rush of gratitude toward this lovely creature. What a sweet, wonderful girl. "I'm uh . . . glad to hear that. My dad is kinda serious. He doesn't joke around. I wasn't sure if that'd go over too good with the kids."

"Well," Naomi assured Ernesto, "I really enjoy the way he teaches. I usually don't even like history, but this term I think it's going to be my favorite class. Well, nice to meet you, Ernesto. Oh, did I tell you, I'm Naomi Martinez."

"Nice to meet you, Naomi," Ernesto mumbled.

"Do your friends call you Ernie?" she asked.

Ernesto thought for a minute that he might tell her the truth, that he didn't have any friends. But he thought better of it. "Yeah, I guess so," he replied.

"Okay then, Ernie, see you around," Naomi said, heading off for her next class. Ernesto watched her, her sweet little figure swaying gently. "Man," Ernesto thought, "she's so cute, so nice . . ."

Abel finally appeared. "Boy dude," he exclaimed, "you like to skate on thin ice, don't you?"

"*What?*" Ernesto asked.

"Getting chummy with Aguirre's chick," Abel said with a grin.

"I wasn't getting chummy with her dude," Ernesto protested. "I was just surprised when she came along and apologized for Aguirre being so rude to me. You could have picked me up off the floor."

Abel was in Ernesto's math class. But in his last two classes of the day, history and speech, Ernesto didn't know anybody. He waited eagerly for the last bell of the day and his chance to break out of the school for home.

Ernesto's parents had rented a house near the high school, and it was easy for him to walk home. Next week he was going to go down to the Department of Motor Vehicles to get his driver's license. He had taken driver's ed in school. His dad had taken him out to practice in empty parking lots on Sunday mornings. Ernesto was hoping for a part-time job and earning enough money to buy an old car. He longed for the freedom that a car would give him.

On his way home from school, Ernesto stopped by Hortencia's restaurant and tamale shop. She was Dad's youngest sister, thirty-one years old and unmarried. She was pretty, with many boyfriends, but she wasn't ready to settle down yet. Hortencia Sandoval was five feet, six inches and attractive. She was turning down guys all the time. Hortencia loved to dance and gamble at the local casinos. One time, when Ernesto's parents went to a party, Ernesto couldn't believe that Hortencia danced the flamenco like a professional, her black hair flying.

"Hey Ernie!" Hortencia called out. "Hungry for a tamale? I made some fresh."

"Just a taco and a soda," Ernesto replied.

"So how is school going, *muchacho*?" *Tía* Hortencia asked as she brought the taco with a side salad.

"So far I'm kinda lost," Ernesto answered. "I don't know anybody but one guy. I feel like a stranger."

"Coming into a school when you're sixteen years old is tough, Ernie," Hortencia sympathized. "But give it time. You'll make some great friends. Trust me, *muchacho*. In a few weeks you'll have a lot of friends."

"I wish we coulda stayed in LA," Ernesto sighed. "I liked that school up there. But when Dad got cut, we had no choice but to come here."

"I hear you, Ernie. I don't know what this world is coming to. Cutting teachers and cops like they're doing. They're tearing the whole community apart," Hortencia declared indignantly. "The athletes are making millions of bucks. Yet they begrudge the people who're teaching our kids and keeping us safe a few measly dollars. I don't get it. It's *loco*. But you'll be okay, Ernie. Your father was just like you when he was a teenager. He was a loner. He wasn't a big hit with the chicks. Then he met your mama, and it was like fireworks in July, baby. You'll find some pretty *muchacha* too, Ernie."

Ernesto smiled at his aunt. *Tía* Hortencia was just about his favorite relative except for *Abuela* Lena. You couldn't stay down-hearted with Hortencia around.

"I'm looking for a part-time job," Ernie told his aunt. "You know anybody who's hiring? I need to buy a cheap little car."

"I'd hire you here, Ernie," Hortencia replied. "But I don't need anybody right now. Go down the street and try the pizzeria. I heard Bashar was hiring. He's a good guy too."

"Thanks," Ernie said, finishing his taco and heading down to the pizzeria.

When Ernesto went inside the pizzeria, he was glad to see some Latino faces. "Hello," he told the guy at the counter, "I'm a junior at Cesar Chavez High and I need a part-time job."

The man handed Ernesto an application and said, "Fill it out and come back tomorrow when the boss is in." Ernesto took the application, stuffed it into his binder, and continued toward home. His father would be home much later. When Dad worked up in Los Angeles, he was always the last teacher to go home. Even after class ended, he'd stay at his desk in case a student wanted to talk. When a kid was having trouble—no matter what kind—Luis Sandoval was ready to listen and help if he could. Ernesto knew that high school dropouts broke his father's heart.

"It's like shutting the door on their whole future," he lamented. "Being fifteen or sixteen and having no dreams, no hope for tomorrow! They're young with their whole lives ahead of them, and they give up." Luis Sandoval was proud of many things he had done. He got the greatest satisfaction from the kids he had turned around. These were the ones getting ready to drop out and who instead stayed in school and graduated.

"He's a good teacher and a good man," Ernesto thought to himself as he walked home. Ernesto was proud of his father for many reasons. Dad was unfailingly kind, even when he himself was tired and discouraged. You could always see his love. You could always see that he cared, that he didn't do or say anything out of anger or meanness. Ernesto felt so anxious that maybe those *bobos* at Chavez High wouldn't appreciate the treasure they had in Luis Sandoval.

"Hey Mom!" Ernesto cried as he came in the house. He heard Katalina and Juanita giggling in the front room. They were always happy. Ernesto thought it was great to be six and eight years old. His sisters believed everything was okay and would always be okay, no matter what was going on. Ernesto remembered feeling like that himself when he was that age.

Then one day, when he was eleven, that feeling ended. Dad got a phone call that his father had suddenly died. Ernesto watched his father standing by the telephone, his face ashen, tears streaming down his cheeks. His dad's look was the most terrible sight Ernesto had ever seen. It was like watching a strong, broad tree that had always stood tall crumble and fall before his eyes. Ernesto had never thought that anything could make his tall, strong father lean against the doorframe and sob like a child. Ernesto was struck with horror, by shock, and then by his own grief. He thought the world had come to an end.

In the next few somber, sad days, the prayers and the funeral and the burial all followed. Ernesto's sisters were too young to understand any of it, but Ernesto was not too young to know and to suffer. And at that time, when he was only eleven, he lost his belief that everything was going to turn out all right and that nothing truly terrible would ever happen.

And last spring, another blow fell on the family and on Ernesto's sense of security. His father had come home from the school to announce that, due to budget cutbacks, he would not be returning to his teaching position in the fall. Ernesto watched Mom sit down quickly at the kitchen table, her eyes wide, her face pale.

Many days and weeks of job hunting, of sending out applications for other teaching jobs, followed. Ernesto could see the fear growing in both his parents even though they tried to hide it from him. It had occurred to them that there might not be another position. They were asking themselves, "What then?"

Then one Friday afternoon Dad came home clutching a very thick envelope. The high school in the *barrio*, where he used to live, was sending him a contract, which he was holding up in the envelope. He had been interviewed, and the administrators had decided to hire him to teach American and world history. He would be joining the staff at Cesar Chavez High School in the *barrio* where he was born and raised. The whole family felt as though dark clouds were parting and the sun was blazing through. The atmosphere turned festive, as if Christmas had come in March. After ten years of being away, the Sandovals were going home. Dad could now see his mother and his sisters and brothers more frequently. Ernesto's parents could connect with old friends. But most of all, Dad had a job. Hope had returned to his eyes.

That was last spring. Now, Ernesto started his homework. He didn't have many friends to hang with yet.

Ernesto looked up from his books. Since the first day of classes, Ernesto wondered whether things were going well for Dad at Chavez. Every night, he waited nervously for his father to come home, and he hoped Dad had had a good day. But Mom had not asked Dad how things were going, and Luis Sandoval never said. Mom never spoke her fears—not when Ernesto could hear her anyway. Ernesto was sure that she had them. The fear was like a little dark cloud floating in the lovely blue color of her eyes. Ernesto wanted to ask his father. But he knew that Dad would only assure him that things were going well.

At four-thirty, Dad came home. Today, for some reason, Mom seemed anxious to hear about his day.

CHAPTER TWO

"How was your day, Luis?" Mom asked in a cheerful voice.

Dad smiled and said, "Good! But a nice hot cup of coffee would still be welcome, *querida mia*."

Mom laughed. When Dad called her a pet name, everything was all right. Mom made him the strong coffee he liked and brought it to him where he was sitting in the living room. When he sat down, his little girls came running to him with tales of their daily activities, and he listened with interest. Ernesto watched in wonderment and admiration as his father seemed to be interested in the inane details of his girls' day.

"Papa, a man with animals came to our room, and he had a snake," Katalina reported, wide-eyed. "And I held the snake, and I wasn't scared or anything. It felt nice, like soft leather."

Not to be outdone, Juanita crowed, "We had a puppet show, and I got to play the witch. Ms. French said I was scary."

Dad laughed. "Well, my little princesses both had exciting days."

Later on, Ernesto heard his father talking to Mom in the kitchen. "I got through telling the kids about the voyages of exploration. Now we get to the Native American cultures the explorers found here. I always enjoy teaching that part, and the students seem to like it too. I like my classes, Maria. Some really great kids and the rest . . . well, we'll bring them along."

After a long silence, Mom said, "Your sister Magda called today, Luis." Her voice was tense, but she tried very hard not to be alarming.

Magda was Dad's oldest sister. *Abuela* Lena—Dad's mom—lived with Magda and her husband since becoming a widow five years ago. Now Magda was close to fifty.

"Oh?" Dad replied.

"Your mother almost fell this morning," Mom reported.

"Oh!" Dad reacted sharply. "Is she all right?"

"Yes, she's fine Luis," Mom assured him. "But Magda said she's getting frail. She's seventy-five now, and Magda and Henry still work. Magda said she's getting uneasy about leaving her in the house all day. The arrangement worked fine when *Abuela* was hardy, but now . . . " There was genuine worry in Mom's voice.

"Magda has been so wonderful with Mama," Dad mused.

"Yes. Luis, I said I'd talk to you," Mom replied.

"Yes?" Dad asked. "What do you think we should do?"

"We could bring her here," Mom suggested. "We have plenty of room. *Abuela* could stay with us. The den could be fixed up as a little apartment. It has a nice bathroom. I'm home with the children anyway, and I could take her to the store or to the doctor if she needs to go. It would be fine, Luis. I like her very much. We've always gotten along fine. The girls would love to have her here.

They always have so much fun with her playing games . . . ”

Ernesto could not hear his father’s reply or even if he said anything at all. But Ernesto could imagine what was happening. Dad was taking Mom in his arms and kissing her.

His homework done, Ernesto filled out the application for the pizzeria job. He decided to take it down there right now and not wait until tomorrow. It wasn’t dark yet. He could walk down there and deliver the application. He was eager to get the job nailed down.

As Ernesto hurried down the street, he glanced up at the sky. The moon was a thin crescent in the darkening heaven, and near it was Venus. Years ago, Dad had pointed out many objects in the sky to Ernesto. Venus was often close to the moon, and it made a beautiful sight. Ernesto loved science. Ernesto’s science teacher in Los Angeles said he had a scientific mind. He thought he would go into science as his life's work, but he wasn't sure exactly where he would fit in.

Ernesto was almost at the pizzeria when he glanced down the street and noticed a lot of people, mostly young, milling around. Some of them were regular kids, just hanging out, but some were probably gang-bangers or homeless. This neighborhood was not as good as where the Sandovals lived in Los Angeles. Mom's parents had said so when the family decided to move. But there was no choice.

Ernesto went into the pizzeria and said "Hi" to the guy behind the counter. "I know you said to bring the application back tomorrow, but I finished it and . . ."

"Yeah," the man said gruffly. He grabbed the application. Then he turned and yelled, "Bashar! That kid is here about the job. The one I was telling you about."

A heavyset dark man appeared. He had piercing, dark eyes, and a prominent hawk-like nose. "You wanna work here, kid?" he asked.

"Yes sir," Ernesto replied. "I need a part-time job for after school and weekends if you need me. I'm a good worker. I'm getting my driver's license next week, and I need the money to buy a car."

Bashar's stern dark face broke into a grin. He laughed. He was a fat man, and his belly shook when he laughed. "You kids can't wait for wheels." He looked quickly at the application, then he looked up. "Are you honest?" he asked, looking stern again.

"Oh yes, sir. I'm very honest," Ernesto responded.

Bashar laughed again. "Like you're gonna admit it if you're a big crook, kid." He shrugged then. "Okay then, we'll try you out. Come around four tomorrow after school. We'll see if you can work the counter. Then later on maybe you can help make the pizza. Okay? The job is four to nine on Mondays, Wednesdays, and Fridays. Minimum wage. That okay?"

"Oh that's great," Ernesto exclaimed. "Thank you very much. I'll be here. You won't be sorry you're giving me a chance. I worked at the fair last summer, and I helped run a cotton candy concession—and we sold hot dogs too."

Bashar laughed again. "I like you—" He looked at the application. "I like you, Ernesto Sandoval," he said.

Ernesto hurried from the pizzeria, feeling a sense of joy and excitement. He felt better at this moment than at any time since coming to town. He had a job. He was going to make money. It wouldn't be much money, but it was money and all his. His parents told him he could keep his wages.

As Ernesto sprinted down the dark street toward home, he never saw the guys emerge from the shadows behind him. They came up on him, and one of them grabbed him, holding his arm around Ernesto's neck.

"Take it easy, man," a strange, harsh voice told him. "Don't struggle, or I'm gonna crush your windpipe, man. We wanna know what gang you belong to."

"None," Ernesto gasped, his joy of moments ago dissolving into terror.

"You 18th Street, man?" another voice demanded.

"No, no!" Ernesto groaned. Fear had turned him numb. He thought he was going to die. He had no feeling in his arms or legs.

"So this is how it all ends for me?" he thought.

"I'm not 18th Street," Ernesto protested in a voice made raspy by his fear. "I never been in a gang. My folks don't stand for stuff like that."

Ernesto didn't know what to expect next. A knife in his back? The arm around his neck tightening so much he couldn't breathe? He began to pray like *Abuela* prayed—*Madre de Dios,* help me!

Suddenly the guy with his arm around Ernesto's neck released him, giving him a violent shove. Ernesto stumbled forward and fell to his knees. His right knee hit rough concrete, and he got a bloody abrasion. His jeans were torn, and his knee leaked blood. Ernesto got slowly to his feet. He felt shaky, but he was all right. He began to run the rest of the way home. The crescent moon and Venus were still beautiful in the sky, but he paid no attention to them. Nothing was beautiful anymore.

All of a sudden, everything was dark and dirty and dangerous. Ernesto heard the distant wail of a police car's siren, adding to his fear. He ran faster.

Back in Los Angeles, Ernesto had tried out for track, but the coach said he wasn't fast enough. If the guy could have seen him running now he might have changed his mind. Ernesto ran so fast that the stores and then the houses alongside him were just blurs. When he saw the tract house his family rented, he turned up the walk, finally slowing down.

CHAPTER THREE

The family was in the living room. They were watching a nature program about pandas. Katalina and Juanita had fallen in love with pandas now that the local zoo was breeding them.

Ernesto stood in the darkened hallway getting his breath. His chest ached, and his heart was still pounding. He didn't realize until now that his T-shirt was wet with perspiration.

"That you, Ernie?" Dad called out.

"Yeah, Dad, I'm taking a shower," Ernesto called back. He staggered toward the bathroom, pulling his soaking T-shirt over his head as he edged in. He wouldn't tell his parents what had happened tonight.

He would just make them worry. What good would it do to tell them? Ernesto would take his shower, get into clean clothes, and tell them the good news that he had a job.

In science class the next day, Ernesto was sitting at his desk when a girl behind him said, "Dude, you got long legs."

Ernesto turned to see a pretty girl with brown curls and the biggest pale brown eyes he had ever seen. "I guess so," he replied.

"How tall are you?" she asked.

"I think I'm about six one now, but I'm still growing," Ernesto answered.

"With those long legs I bet you go out for track," she remarked.

"I did at my last school, but coach turned me down," Ernesto said.

"I'm Carmen Ibarra," the girl announced. "Everybody says I talk too much, but I don't care. I've got a lot to say. I think talking is the funnest thing in the whole world. Mom talks too much too. We drive Dad crazy. He goes out and hides in the car." The girl laughed. She had a big laugh for such a slender girl. "Hey, what's your name?"

"Ernesto Sandoval," Ernesto told her.

"You gotta go out for the track team here at Chavez, Ernie," she advised. "Our track team is so lame. You never saw such a bunch of losers. I'm telling you, when we go off campus to a meet, everybody is so glad to see us 'cause they know they can beat us. We need a guy like you with long legs. I bet you're a great sprinter. Man, you shoulda seen Chavez against Pat Henry. They were laughing at us, I swear. Poor Coach Muñoz is ready to quit. You gotta go see him, Ernie. You free Tuesday after school? That's when they practice, if you can call what they do practicing."

"I work at the pizzeria, but I guess I'm free Tuesdays," Ernesto replied.

"Great, then you can go see Coach Muñoz," Carmen urged him. "You can try out. He'll take you, Ernie, I swear. I mean my grandmother runs faster than most of the guys on that team. Go for it Ernie. Oh, here comes our science teacher. He's so fun. He's the funnest science teacher I ever had. Did you know that Mr. Escalante is part Filipino? He brings his lunch every day. *Pancit*. Every day. He's so cute. He's about three feet tall. He told me a coupla times that I talk too much, but he was nice about it."

Mr. Escalante was a short dark man of at least five foot five and perhaps more. He smiled at the class and set a plastic container in his desk drawer. It contained his *pancit* for lunch.

"Exciting news," Mr. Escalante announced with a big smile.

"School's been cancelled!" a boy named Eddie Gonzales called out.

"No, but you got another bad mark in my book, Eddie," Mr. Escalante retorted, still smiling. "The exciting news is that a new planet has been discovered. It is close enough to Earth to be studied by our telescopes."

"Can we move there if the earth gets ruined by all the pollution?" Carmen asked.

"Excuse me, Carmen," Mr. Escalante replied. "I did not see you raise your hand before you asked the question."

"Oh sorry," Carmen said, raising her hand. "So can we move to the new planet if we mess up too bad around here?"

"I'm afraid not. It is too hot there," Mr. Escalante explained.

"We could put in air conditioning," Carmen said.

"Again you did not raise your hand, Carmen," Mr. Escalante declared. "Air conditioning wouldn't work. It is four hundred degrees Fahrenheit, and that is much too hot for us. The new planet is a dark dank place filled with hot steam."

This time Carmen raised her hand. "If it's such a dump, why do we even care about it?" she asked.

"Because it is interesting to study," Mr. Escalante explained. "Also, if we found this planet, there is a good chance we shall find others more habitable for humans perhaps."

Science was Ernesto's last class of the day. When it ended, Carmen turned to Ernesto. "What time do you have to be at that pizza place to work?"

"Four o'clock," Ernesto replied.

"Oh," Carmen declared. "Then we got time to run over to Hortencia's for a taco and a soda. She is amazing. The food there is awesome. Come on!"

As they crossed the street to Hortencia's, Ernesto announced, "She's my aunt."

"Get outta here!" Carmen cried. "Hortencia is your aunt?"

"Yeah," Ernesto explained. "*Abuela* was kinda old when she was born. *Abuela* called Hortencia, her *milagra*. She's my dad's sister. She's the youngest of five children."

"Oh that is so cool, Ernie," Carmen cooed. "Everybody loves Hortencia. She is so fun, and she plays the guitar. She's like a mother hen if a kid has a problem. Oh, hey Ernie, you got a girlfriend?"

Ernesto felt his face turn warm. Even in middle school a lot of guys had girlfriends, but he didn't. Nor did he have any girlfriends in freshman year at high school in Los Angeles. Then, when he was a sophomore, he got to be friends with Gabriella. "I don't have a girlfriend right now," he admitted.

"I don't have a boyfriend either," Carmen said, smiling happily. "I had one, but he said I talked too much. Boys are so rude. They aren't interested when you want to tell them stuff. He ditched me, dropped me like a hot potato. Ernie I'll be your girlfriend, and you can be my boyfriend until we find real ones, okay?" Her smile was nearly irresistible.

Ernesto had to laugh and say, "Sure, why not?"

Ernesto felt a little dizzy but happy too. As he walked with Carmen, several other students walked along, all of them on their way to Hortencia's. Ernesto felt as though he belonged here at Cesar Chavez High

School, at least a little bit. The kids walking in the group smiled at him, as if they knew him even though they didn't. Ernesto felt like part of something, at least for now. And he felt good.

Ernesto had his taco and soda with Carmen and the other kids. By the time he had to leave for work at the pizzeria, he felt energized. The summer before, when he worked at the fair, he did well with the customers; so he thought he'd handle his new job okay too.

When Ernesto got to the pizzeria, he stood at the counter with an older kid named Ivan. He watched everything Ivan did—how he took orders, how he asked about what they wanted on their pizza, how he served the condiments they liked. Then Ivan let Ernesto take some orders. He got nervous and flubbed only a few times. By the end of the shift, he felt he was doing well, and Ivan gave him a high five. Bashar emerged from the kitchen and slapped Ernesto on the back so hard he almost knocked him over. But the big man said in a friendly voice, "I think we keep you, boy. Yeah, you're okay. See you on Wednesday."

Ernesto put on his jacket and headed into the darkness outside. Ordinarily, he wouldn't have given a second thought to going home a few blocks in the dark. But what happened the other night loomed large in his mind. Going through those few blocks would be like passing through a dark forest, knowing that hungry wolves were among the trees, waiting for prey.

Ernesto tried to tell himself it wouldn't happen again. He had been a stranger, and they'd thought he was from a rival gang. Why would they bother him again when they knew he was just a jerk kid?

Still, Ernesto kept off the main drag and ran home through the alleys. A lot of dogs barked at him as he ran, but, by the time their owners checked, Ernesto was long gone. He ran fast. Carmen was right. He could probably do the track team a lot of good. Being on the track team would be a good way to make friends. Helping the team win a few meets would also be a big boost to Ernesto's ego. He had never had an athletic achievement since playing sandlot baseball as a kid.

Abel Ruiz lived just a block from Ernesto; so they walked to school together the next morning.

"How'd the pizza gig go, man?" Abel asked.

"Good!" Ernesto replied. "I got the hang of it real easy. I like it, Abel. It makes me happy to think I made a few bucks too. The boss, Bashar, he's real good about sharing the proceeds form the tip jar with everybody too. So that's extra money."

Ernesto remembered that today was Tuesday and that he was going to try out for the track team after classes.

"This girl, Carmen Ibarra," Ernesto confided in Abel, "she's in science with me. She talked me into seeing the coach about being on the track team, Abel."

"Oh yeah, little motormouth. Ain't she a hoot?" Abel laughed. "Cute as a chipmunk too. If only she'd stop talking once in a while."

"I think I'd like to be on the track team," Ernesto remarked, "but maybe I'll get turned down like I was in LA."

"I think Coach Muñoz will grab you. The guy is desperate," Abel assured him. "Good move for you too, man. Chicks like athletes."

As they neared the school, Ernesto spotted Naomi Martinez walking alone. Usually she walked with Clay Aguirre. She was wearing another pretty top, this time a pale green. When she pushed the sleeves up, Ernesto noticed an ugly bruise on her forearm. She caught Ernesto looking and pulled down the sleeves. "Man!" Ernesto seethed with sudden anger. "Did you see that bruise on the Naomi's arm?"

"Yeah I did," Abel noted. "She doesn't play sports either. Maybe the girls were doing a cheer routine, and she fell and somebody grabbed her hard or something."

"Or maybe *he* grabbed her in anger," Ernesto snarled.

"Who?" Abel asked.

"You know who I mean. That creep Aguirre," Ernesto snapped.

"Hey man, don't go off half-cocked," Abel advised. "You hear what I'm sayin'? Don't go sticking your nose into no beehive you don't know nothin' about. I've seen Aguirre when he's ticked off. I wouldn't touch him with a ten-foot pole, man."

"Abel," Ernesto declared, "if he got rough with Naomi and bruised her up like that, I'm not going to just look away, man. You don't turn your back on a chick in trouble, not if you like to think you're a man."

"Ernie, listen to me," Abel pleaded. "This isn't the neighborhood where you lived up there in la-la land. This is a tougher, meaner 'hood, man. I'm talking to you like a homie would, man. Naomi is a smart chick. If she's got a problem with her guy, she needs to take care of business her own self. You don't need to be comin' on like some crazy Zorro rescuing the damsel in distress. I like you dude. I don't want to see you walkin' into no buzz saw."

Ernesto turned. "I'm gonna ask Naomi what happened," he announced, walking over to the girl. His eyes were hard and determined. He left Abel muttering to himself and confronted Naomi as she neared English class. "Hey Naomi," he called out.

She smiled. Ernesto wasted no time.

"I noticed you got a bad bruise on your arm. You okay, girl?" Ernesto asked in a businesslike voice, even though he was shaking a little.

Naomi smiled again. She pulled up her sleeve. "Oh this?" she remarked. "Don't remind me. Isn't it awful? I did something really stupid. We got a new dog at home, a pit bull, and he's really strong. I got his chain wrapped around my arm, and he yanked on it. Ouch! He's not a mean dog, but he's playful. He doesn't know his own strength. I thought he'd pull my arm out of the socket! Thanks for being concerned, Ernie. I hope you never get in a tug-of-war with a pit bull! Believe me, he's gonna win!"

"I thought maybe somebody hurt you," Ernesto commented.

"Oh no! Heavens no!" Naomi protested. "But it was sweet of you to worry. You're a nice guy, Ernie."

She looked even more beautiful than she looked yesterday. Ernesto felt like his whole body was electrified or something. Just looking at her made him tingle. The hair stood up on the nape of his neck. "It would really tick me off if some jerk roughed you up," Ernesto remarked, not quite believing her story about the pit bull.

Before Naomi had a chance to answer, Clay Aguirre came walking along with another jock. He glared at Ernesto. "What's with you, freak? You annoying my girl again? Don't you know what 'no' means, stick boy? She's not interested in you. You're not her type." He laughed scornfully at his comment, joined by his companion.

"Oh Clay, knock it off," Naomi protested. "Ernesto and I were just talking about our new pit bull. He's just a puppy, but he's really hard to control."

Clay threw an arm around Naomi's shoulders and said, "He's a *macho* dog. I like that, babe. I like it in animals and people. Nothin' makes me sicker than wimps." At his last remark, he cast Ernesto a sneer.

Ernesto turned on his heel and returned to where Abel was standing.

"You make a fool of yourself, man?" Abel asked sourly.

"I guess so," Ernesto admitted. "Seems like Naomi's family has this new pit bull, and she got his chain wrapped around her arm. That's her story anyway. But you know what, Abel? Chicks lie about stuff like that. Up in LA, there was this girl always showing up to school with bruises and cuts. She kept lying through her teeth about it. Couple of us just confronted her one day and got the truth. She had this lousy abusive boyfriend, and he kept beating on her. She covered for him and kept making up fake stories. But we got the guy busted, and I think maybe we saved her from ending up in the hospital or worse."

"Man, you don't give up, do you?" Abel commented, shaking his head. "The problem here is you got the hots for Naomi and you want to break her up with Clay Aguirre. Come on, admit that's what's going on, man. You want to move in on his chick, and you're looking for ways to do it."

"No," Ernesto asserted. "Sure, she's a beautiful girl, and it'd be great to be with her. But I'm no fool. I know I'm not in her league. I got no illusions, man. It's just that I don't want a chick to be jerked around by some brute."

"I believe her about the dog, Ernie," Abel declared. "She's no fool. She's really into Aguirre, but she wouldn't take abuse from a guy. She's too smart for that. Listen to me, Ernie. Get over it."

"There's nothing to get over, man," Ernesto protested in an annoyed voice. Abel talking like that made him all the madder because what he said was at least partially true. He knew Naomi Martinez was way out of his league, but still in his fantasies he could see himself with her . . .

After classes ended for the day, Ernesto headed for the football field where the track team practiced. As he approached, he saw some guys running, and Carmen had not been far off the mark. They weren't running very well.

"Hi Coach," Ernesto called out. "I'm Ernesto Sandoval, and we just moved here from Los Angeles. I'm a junior. I'd like to try out for the track team if you think it'd be okay. I ran in LA, but I couldn't make the team. I'm a lot better now. I been doing a lot of running."

Coach Muñoz looked the boy up and down, a hopeful expression in his eyes. "You look a little scrawny," Coach remarked, "but you got long legs, Sandoval.

Believe me, we're hungry for talent around here. You any relation to the new history teacher, Luis Sandoval?"

"Yes, he's my dad," Ernesto replied.

"He's a great guy," Coach commented. "Everybody on the staff likes him. Well, we need a lot of help around here, Sandoval. I've got motivated guys, but they're not very good yet. Maybe you heard that when we go out on meets, we get blown out of the box. I'd sure like to put an end to that. You know the drills, the breathing exercises, the way to stretch muscles, how to pump your arms?"

"Yeah," Ernesto affirmed. "I've done all that." Up in LA, Ernesto had just a mild interest in getting on the track team. He had a lot of friends and other things going for him. But around here, he still felt like a stranger. He needed to belong to something like the track team to feel at home. He wanted to be out there on the track running well, maybe with kids cheering. He thought about bringing in a victory and maybe the chicks liking his style. He thought about maybe Naomi Martinez seeing him in a new way.

Ernesto stiffened. He was shocked by what was going through his mind. Abel Ruiz knew him better than he knew himself. He wanted to run not just for himself, but to get Naomi's attention. He wasn't willing to settle for the fact that she was Clay Aguirre's girl, now and always. He wanted a shot at becoming her boyfriend.

As Ernesto did his stretches and warmups, he realized how right Abel was, and the thought irked him. He *did* have the hots for Naomi. He thought about her a lot. He looked for her when he arrived on the campus. He enjoyed seeing what kind of sweater or top she would be wearing.

When he ready to run, Coach Muñoz pulled out his stopwatch. "Okay Sandoval," he said, "let's see what you got. Make my day, kid. Give me some hope for turning this team around. I'm sick and tired of being the laughingstock of the sports department."

Ernesto looked at the man and felt sympathy for him. Coach wasn't young, and he was probably only a few years from finishing his career. Everybody wanted to go out a winner. If things continued as they had been going, Coach Muñoz was destined to go out not in a blaze of glory but in humiliation.

Ernesto stepped up to the starting line and got into position.

"Get set, ready, *go!*" Coach Muñoz said.

Ernesto lunged from the starting line, his arms pumping. Suddenly he wanted to make this team more than he ever wanted anything in a good long time. He knew he was running very fast, and he was delighted.

CHAPTER FOUR

When Ernesto Sandoval completed a lap and saw Coach Muñoz, he noted a big smile breaking out on the man's face.

"You're okay, Sandoval. You got raw talent," Coach Muñoz shouted as Ernesto came running up. Ernesto worked with the coach for another forty-five minutes on muscle stretching techniques and breathing. Then Muñoz signed Ernesto up for the team. Coach gave him some papers for his parents to sign, and he grabbed Ernesto's hand. "I think we got a shot at the one hundred meters with you on the team. I think we could even ace the relays, boy," Muñoz gloated. "You take care of yourself. You eat good and get your rest and do a lot of running, Sandoval."

As he left the field, Ernesto felt pumped. Abel had been watching from the sidelines. Now he shouted, "You looked awesome, dude!"

Another voice chirped out from the sidelines. "You go, Ernie!" Carmen Ibarra was yelling. "I never seen a guy run so fast since some kid vandalized our Christmas decorations and Pop ran after him."

Ernesto grinned at Carmen. "Thanks for coming to see me," he told her. "You gave me a good steer, Carmen. I like Coach. I really enjoy running, and now I guess I'm on the team. I think I can help myself and the team too."

As they left the school grounds, Ernesto told Abel, "I gotta study for my driver's test tonight. I'm going on the computer and find the practice tests. Some of those questions are plain stupid, but some of them are tricky too. I've just been living for getting my driver's license. It's like a ticket to freedom, man. I've saved up about five hundred dollars from birthday and Christmas gifts.

With my pay from the pizza place, I think I can get some wheels pretty soon."

Abel laughed. "The engine may be falling out, but, hey, you can always shove it back in."

"Abel," Ernesto changed the subject. "My grandmother maybe is coming to live with us. She's getting a little feeble. She's been living with my Aunt Magda, but she and her husband work. So maybe *Abuela* Lena will be living with us."

"How do you feel about that, dude?" Abel asked. "I'd hate for my grandma to come live with my family. Mom and Pop are on my case enough without having some ancient lady bossing me around 'cause the world ain't like she remembers when she was young. My grandma complains all the time. It gets me down, man."

"*Abuela* Lena is pretty cool," Ernesto said. "I get along good with her. She likes to go to church a lot. She's always down there at Our Lady of Guadalupe Church, lighting candles and stuff like that. She's not bossy, though. She told my dad he should raise his kids the way he and Mom want, and it's none of her business. She says she had her turn raising kids and making rules, and she doesn't want that no more. Now she just likes playing with my sisters. She's crazy about Katalina and Juanita, and it seems like she never gets tired of playing their dumb games with them."

"That's okay then," Abel agreed. "I guess maybe not all old people are the same."

They passed Hortencia's restaurant and saw two guys from Chavez High hanging out in front. Ernesto sort of recognized their faces, but he didn't know their names. He hadn't learned too many names yet. Abel knew them, though. "Hey Dom, Carlos," he yelled. "I didn't see you guys at school today. You hide in the bushes?"

Dom Reynosa was a short guy with long hair and skin even darker than Ernesto's. He looked like a Native American. Carlos Negrete was thickset, and Ernesto thought he looked like he might be trouble.

"We didn't go to that lockup joint today," Dom exclaimed. "I hate goin' to Chavez. Don't know how much longer I'm showin' up, to tell the truth."

Carlos nodded. He was texting on his phone as he talked. "Teachers're boring old crocks. Who cares about all that junk we're learning? My history teacher, he's so boring he puts me to sleep. He's talking about how the Indians lived in their villages a billion years ago . . . like anybody cares."

Ernesto winced. Just looking at these two guys gave Ernesto the chills. And he feared the guy was talking about his father. He could imagine his father facing a classroom full of these jerks, trying to keep them interested and finding it impossible.

"You're juniors already," Abel protested. "You'd be stupid to quit now. You don't have that diploma, you don't have nothin' man. Nobody wants to hire dropouts. You wanna work dishing up hamburgers and hot dogs all your life?"

"Hey Abel," Dom laughed, "you sound just like that history teacher we got. He's like pushing us to stay in school like his life depended on it."

"He cares about you guys," Ernesto blurted, getting into the conversation. "He knows that *your* lives depend on staying in school and graduating. I know 'cause he's my dad."

Dom and Carlos stared at Ernesto and then said, "Who're you man? You sayin' you're Mr. Sandoval's kid? He's your old man?"

"Yeah," Ernesto replied "Mr. Sandoval is my dad, and he feels bad when his students drop out 'cause he figures he must've failed or something."

"Man, is he as boring at home as he is in the classroom?" Dom asked. "That guy can talk and talk . . . he makes me crazy."

"He's a pretty interesting guy," Ernesto affirmed. "You can learn a lot from him. He's in the National Guard, you know. His unit fought in Iraq. He ever tell you about that?"

Both Dom and Carlos looked surprised. "No way! That dude is a pressed suit. He ain't never seen no battles."

"Yeah, he was a soldier in Iraq," Ernesto asserted.

"He never let on anything about that," Carlos said.

"He doesn't talk about it," Ernesto continued, his heart pounding. "But he was gone for two years. He was in some of the worst places where those IEDs were going off like firecrackers on the Fourth of July." Ernesto was immensely proud of his father. He was proud because his Dad fought bravely in a terrible war and earned a Purple Heart for being seriously wounded. But he was also proud because he was a good and lovable guy who really cared about people, especially his students, even those who hated him. It hurt Ernesto to realize that a lot of these guys looked at Dad as some boring old teacher who had nothing to offer them.

"Hey," Dom remarked, "he's got this funny scar on his right cheek under his eye.

I always thought maybe he was a gang-banger when he was a kid and somebody came at him with a broken bottle or something. Did he get the scar in Iraq?"

"Yeah, an IED almost took out his eye," Ernesto explained.

Ernesto knew his father would be annoyed if he knew his son was telling these guys about his experiences in Iraq. He would have been mortified that Ernesto was bragging up his war record to impress his students, but Ernesto didn't care. These punks needed to know just whom they were dissing.

Across the street from Hortencia's, new graffiti had appeared on the fence. This time, somebody had painted a pouncing puma. It was bright yellow with a gaping red mouth. Ernesto had to admit it was pretty good art. Carlos saw Ernesto looking at it, and he asked, "What do you think of that, man?"

"It's not bad," Ernesto commented.

Carlos grinned. "Me and Dom did that," he announced. "We're taggers. That's what

Dom's doin' right now, texting the guys so we know where to meet tonight. We even hang out with some gangbangers. They're pretty cool, man."

"That's stupid," Ernesto snapped. "Gangbangers are stupid idiots who shoot people. Up in LA one time, they were shooting at each other, and a little kid got in the middle. They put down a three-year-old kid."

Anger flared in the eyes of both boys, and Ernesto felt as though he had to smooth things over. "But the art *is* pretty good," he said. "It sorta reminds me of murals I've seen in Mexico. We went down there one time and saw murals by famous dudes, and your stuff reminds me of that."

"Yeah?" Carlos asked, his chest puffing out a little.

"Looks like the stuff Rivera and Orozco did," Ernesto remarked.

Carlos and Dom looked at each other. Then Dom asked, "Who are those guys?"

"They taggers?" Carlos wondered.

Abel laughed out loud, and Dom took an aggressive step toward him. "You want a busted face, dude?" Dom asked. Abel backpedaled.

"They're Mexican artists from the last century," Ernesto stated. "José Orozco painted murals with a message. Big, dramatic murals. And then Diego Rivera, he used these bright colors that really grab your attention."

Carlos looked hard at Ernesto. "Who told you about these guys?" he asked. "I never heard of them. You ain't just making them up, are you, man?"

"My father told me," Ernesto explained. "He's interested in everything, history, music, art. Do either of you guys take art?"

The boys looked at each other and laughed. "Last time I had an art class was kindergarten when we did fingerpainting," Dom said.

"Yeah and some old lady had us making angels outta pasta," Carlos added.

"You oughta take art," Ernesto urged them. "I heard that Ms. Polk at Chavez High is good."

"Ahhh, it'd be just a waste of time," Dom protested.

"Well," Ernesto said, "good meeting you guys."

They exchanged fist bumps, and Carlos said a little grudgingly, "You're okay, Sandoval."

As they neared home, Ernesto said to Abel, "Those are the kind of dudes my poor dad has to put up with. They don't want to be in school."

"You did pretty good with them back there, Ernie," Abel remarked. "Why don't you tell your father they're taggers. You know, maybe he could get the school to let them do a mural. We got a lot of ugly blank places at Chavez."

"Hey Abel, that's a good idea!" Ernesto agreed.

When Ernesto reached his house, he saw *Tía* Magda's car in the driveway.

When he got inside the house, he heard *Abuela*'s soft voice and *Tía* Magda's spirited voice.

"I don't know, Maria," *Abuela* was saying, "I'm happy at my daughter's house, and I'm pretty healthy. That fall was just because I got careless. I use a cane now."

"We'd love to have you here, Mama," Ernesto's mother urged. "The girls would be so happy if you were here, and we could fix up the den for you. You really need to think about it."

"Mama," Magda added, "we just worry about you being alone in the house all day . . ."

"You're such a sweetheart, Maria," *Abuela* said. "I always tell Luis he found a girl as beautiful on the inside as she is on the outside."

"Oh Mama," Ernesto's mother laughed. "You should hear me nagging Luis about leaving his clothes strewn all over the house. And we fight about politics too. He is much more liberal than I am."

Ernesto came into the living room and gave his grandmother a hug. "I hope you come here with us, *Abuela*," he said.

Ernesto then went to his room to study online for the DMV test. He studied the speed limits in various places. In school zones you could go no faster than twenty-five miles an hour. Ernesto thought the speed limit would be even lower. Ernesto knew he'd be a cautious driver like his father. He thought if he made any mistakes on the written test, it would be because he thought speeds would be lower.

"Hey Ernie, watcha doin'?" Katalina asked, coming into his room.

"Hey Kat. I'm studying for my driver's test," Ernesto replied.

"You really gonna drive?" the little girl asked.

"I hope so," Ernesto said.

"You gonna drive our minivan?" Katalina asked. The family had just one car, and it was old.

"I'm gonna get a car of my own if I can," Ernesto answered.

"You gotta get a red car," Katalina declared. "A red sports car. Then you can keep the top down. I love red cars. When I grow up, I'm gonna get a red sports car."

"I'll be lucky to get some old junker," Ernesto laughed. He looked at his little sister. She was already beautiful. In a few years the boys would be noticing her. Ernesto felt his back stiffen. He would have to look out for his little sister. No creeps better take advantage of her. He felt sorry for the dude who tried to have his way with his little sister.

When Luis Sandoval came home from school, Ernesto went out to talk to him. "You got a minute, Dad?" he asked.

"Sure," Dad replied as he swung his legs from the minivan.

"I met a couple of your students today, me and Abel did. Dom Reynosa and Carlos Negrete," Ernesto said.

Dad winced. "I imagine they had some choice things to say about their boring old teacher," he suggested.

"Yeah, well, they're taggers, you know," Ernesto said.

"Wonderful," Dad nodded, shuddering. "Another asset."

"Dad," Ernesto persisted, "we saw some of the stuff they painted on a fence. It was good. Abel thought you might recruit them to do a mural on one of the blank walls at school. I told them about famous Mexican muralists like Rivera, and their eyes sort of lit up. You know what, Dad? That might make them stay in school."

Luis Sandoval smiled. "Ernie, that's brilliant!" he said enthusiastically. "Thank Abel for his idea and thank you too. I'll talk to Ms. Polk, and we'll get on it right away. We could get a bunch of kids like that together and . . . that's just a great idea."

Ernesto grinned at his father. He knew he'd go for the idea. Anything that could be done to keep kids in the classroom until they graduated was precious to Dad. Ernesto could remember his father often sitting at the kitchen table, lamenting over another kid who had dropped out of school. Luis Sandoval had gone to school in this *barrio,* and he'd seen many of his own friends drop out before graduation.

But now, as Dad thought of getting his two students to do the mural, he was as excited as a child. In a way, by rescuing Dom and Carlos, Dad seemed to feel he was somehow reclaiming the past.

CHAPTER FIVE

At school the next day, Ernesto spotted Naomi and Clay walking together. Every once in a while they stopped, and Naomi looked up adoringly at Clay. Once he kissed her. The sight of that made Ernesto sick. She deserved better. Why couldn't she see that? Ernesto didn't care what Abel said about minding his own business. He hated to see a nice girl like Naomi stuck on a creep. But he didn't know how to tell her without coming off as a jealous creep himself. Ernesto still did not believe the pit bull story. He was sure Clay had gotten angry at Naomi, grabbed her wrist too tightly, and bruised her. Ernesto was sure Clay had grabbed her lovely, small arm with those big, brutal hands of his . . . Ernesto felt his own hands tightening. He wanted to punch Clay Aguirre out, as stupid and impossible as doing that was.

Ernesto had illusions that he could protect Naomi from Clay.

"Dude, give it up," urged a voice behind Ernesto. Ernesto turned to see Abel frowning at him.

"Give what up?" Ernesto asked as if he didn't know.

"Looking at that chick," Abel insisted. "She's crazy in love with the creep. Stop thinking you're going to ride up on your white horse and save her from herself. It ain't gonna happen. She doesn't want for it to happen. Don't fall for her man, not anymore than you already have."

"You're all wet, dude," Ernesto protested and then changed the subject. "Oh, by the way, I told Dad about your idea to get Dom and Carlos into doing a school mural, and he loved the idea. He's gonna get something started today. Dad is really anxious to keep the guys in school any way he can. He's on a one-man crusade to conquer the dropout problem in the *barrio*."

"*Muy bien,* man!" Abel cried.

As they approached Ms. Hunt's classroom, they both heard Clay Aguirre's angry voice exploding in the quiet morning air just outside the door to the building.

"*Where is it!?*" he was screaming at Naomi.

Ernesto could see that Naomi was flipping madly through her binder in search of something. She seemed almost hysterical. Then she looked up and said, "Oh Clay, I must have left it at home!"

"You said you'd bring the report," Clay screamed. "It has to be turned in in five minutes! You stupid little moron. You idiot! *Damn you!*"

"I'm sorry, Clay," Naomi moaned. "*I'm so sorry . . .*"

Ernesto's muscles tightened. Every nerve in his body got ready for action. Clay Aguirre looked so furious he seemed about to slap

Naomi across her face. But Ernesto was going to stop him if he made one move toward hurting the girl. Ernesto was going to grab Clay and drag him away. He wasn't going to stand by and watch Naomi get hurt. He didn't care about the consequences. If the school busted him for fighting, so be it.

But Ms. Hunt had entered the classroom and was getting ready to start class. Clay glared at Naomi, thought better of doing anything stupid, and stomped past Ernesto and Abel into the classroom. Naomi followed close behind him.

Ms. Hunt had assigned a two-page report to her students, and she said the only excuse for not turning it in on time that she would accept would be if the student had died. She was joking, of course, but the excuse for not turning in the report had to be very good. Clay Aguirre's explaining that his girlfriend was supposed to do the work for him but that she forgot to bring it in wouldn't cut it.

Ernesto wondered why the jerk hadn't written his own report. Maybe he didn't have time what with football practice and all. He'd palmed the work off on Naomi, and she mistakenly left it at home.

Clay strode into the classroom ahead of Naomi and went to Ms. Hunt's desk as she was sitting down. "Ms. Hunt," he pleaded, "I swear I did that report, but then I left it at home this morning. So I'm wondering if—"

Naomi didn't say anything. Ashen-faced, she took her seat.

"I'm sorry, Clay, that's just no excuse," Ms. Hunt replied. "You'll have to take an F for the assignment because you didn't turn it in."

"Uh, listen," Clay continued standing at the teacher's desk. "There was so much going on at my house this morning, I just left it sitting there at the computer. But I swear I did it, and it was really good too."

"No luck," Ms. Hunt insisted. "Sorry, Clay. Please be seated so I can pick up the reports and start class."

"Ms. Hunt, see," Clay persisted. He was worrying about his grade in this class if he got an F for the assignment. He was close to losing his football eligibility.

"Clay," Ms. Hunt said, "you are really annoying me now. Sit down and I mean it." Ms. Hunt no longer looked anything like the jovial teacher she usually was, the one who enjoyed bantering with her students. As Clay returned to his desk, he shot Naomi a withering look.

Naomi looked down, awash in regret. She seemed near tears. Ernesto was so angry he could barely focus on the class. Naomi probably thought she was in love with this creep. "How could anyone who loved you treat you like this?" Ernesto wondered. He was afraid for Naomi. He thought about a girl he had known up in Los Angeles who was almost seriously beaten by her boyfriend. What would Clay do when they were alone today with no watching?

"Here we have one of the most powerful scenes in *Macbeth,*" Ms. Hunt began, bringing Ernesto's attention back to the class. "A doctor enters the room to describe the strange behavior of Lady Macbeth. What is she doing to alarm those around her?"

Ernesto raised his hand. "She's walking around in her sleep," he answered. "Her eyes are open, but she's asleep. And she's rubbing her hands like she's washing them, over and over."

"Yes," Ms. Hunt affirmed. "And what is causing her to act in that way?"

"She's trying to wash blood off her hands," Ernesto replied. "She thinks she has blood on her hands because she's feeling guilty about the murder. Her guilt over her part in the murder is giving her this idea that she's got blood on her hands."

"Yes," Ms. Hunt replied, looking out at the class. "Listen to these haunting words, 'what will these hands ne're be clean?' "

Carmen Ibarra raised her hand and quoted from the play. "And she goes, 'here's the smell of blood still. All the perfumes of Arabia will not sweeten this little hand. Oh, oh, oh.' "

"And this is what makes Shakespeare so striking, so powerful," Ms. Hunt declared. "He plumbs the depths of human emotion. We watch these TV dramas, and people kill each other. But you rarely see any remorse, any sense of guilt. The story focuses entirely on catching the culprit and on the person trying to get away. Shakespeare shows us true human reactions to terrible events. The players feel guilt and regret. In this case, there's so much guilt that it leads to madness. When real human beings commit these terrible crimes, they feel guilt unless they're complete sociopaths, as few people, even few murderers, are. This is why we study Shakespeare and why his work is such a rich and rewarding experience."

Ernesto was fascinated by Ms. Hunt's enthusiasm for her subject. He thought she was a great teacher. For a few minutes, he even forgot about Naomi and her problem.

Usually when English class ended, Naomi and Clay walked out together, talking and laughing or holding hands. This time

Clay bounded out of the classroom alone, leaving Naomi behind. She forlornly slipped on her cardigan sweater, picked up her binder, and got up. Ernesto was tempted to walk over to her and say something. But what could he say? "I'm real sorry your boyfriend is such a creep. Maybe you should think of dropping him, Naomi. In case you do, just remember I'm here for you." Ernesto grimaced mentally at the very idea he might say such a thing. He stood in silence as she slowly walked out of the classroom in a daze, like a zombie.

All that day, Ernesto kept an eye out for Naomi. She usually had lunch with Clay in a grassy little clearing just behind the library. Benches and tables were there. But instead she just went to one of the vending machines, bought a nutrition bar, and ate it as she walked away. She stopped for a few minutes to watch Ms. Polk and some boys measuring the wall of the science building. Ernesto recognized Dom and Carlos. They were beginning to make plans for the mural.

Ernesto was planning to go home. He wanted to get some homework done before he had to leave for work. But then he saw Naomi starting down the street alone, and he caught up with her.

"Do you live close enough to school to walk home?" he asked her. He'd seen her riding home with Clay most days.

"Oh sure. I like to walk," Naomi offered a limp smile. "You live close too, Ernie?"

"Yeah, I just walk down Washington. Then I turn on Tremayne, and my street is four blocks down. Wren Street," Ernesto replied.

"I guess you pass my street then. I live on Bluebird Street," Naomi offered.

"Then we can walk together most of the way," Ernesto suggested.

"Sure," Naomi agreed. "You might want to come down to my house for a couple minutes and meet Brutus."

"Who's Brutus?" Ernesto asked.

"Our new pit bull. Dad named him Brutus," Naomi answered.

Ernesto was surprised. So there really was a pit bull. At least that part of the story was true. But he still thought Naomi made up the dog story as a cover for what Clay had done to her.

"We don't have a dog," Ernesto said. "We have a cat, though. Her name is Calico."

"Don't you like dogs, Ernie?" Naomi asked, turning to look at him with her amazing violet eyes. Ernesto got instant goose bumps. He could feel the little hairs popping up on his arms. A shiver went up Ernesto's spine. Abel was right on the money. Ernesto was falling for her. He couldn't stop himself anymore than a guy falling off a cliff could stop himself. "Oh yeah, we've had dogs," Ernesto responded. "We haven't got around to replacing our golden retriever. He died in LA. So . . . uh, you guys like pit bulls?"

Ernesto couldn't imagine anybody wanting a pit bull. He never really knew a pit bull well, but he heard all the scary stories about them. He figured you'd have to be weird to want one. Maybe the dogs were really nice if they were raised with kindness, but Ernesto didn't want to test the theory.

"My father wanted one," Naomi explained. "He loves big, aggressive dogs. Dad is sorta like that himself. He's very forceful. He's a fork lift operator. Very macho. He's a big guy. He's very good at what he does."

As they turned onto Bluebird, Ernesto saw the green stucco house with the red tile roof. "There's our place," Naomi pointed. "Only green house on the street. Every other house is mocha or white or something." Even though she smiled often as she spoke, Naomi looked sad. Ernesto figured she was still feeling bad about the trouble with Clay.

"Come on in for a few minutes," Naomi suggested. "Mom made brownies last night. She makes the best brownies."

"You sure?" Ernesto asked. He wondered whether Clay was hiding across the street behind the eucalyptus trees.

"Absolutely," Naomi assured him. "Come on." She led the way up the walk.

When they reached the door, a fierce-looking white dog was barking furiously behind the screen door. He was lunging toward the door as if he wanted to get out and deal personally with the visitors. It was the biggest, meanest-looking pit bull Ernesto had ever seen.

"Brutus!" a man growled from within the house. "Get back in here." The dog backed away from the door, and a burly man with dark curly hair appeared. He wore a T-shirt that couldn't quite cover his large stomach. He glared at Ernesto. Ernesto didn't know who scared him more, the pit bull or this guy.

"Papa," Naomi began, "this is Ernesto Sandoval from school. His dad is my American history teacher. He's awesome."

"Hey," Mr. Martinez said. "Your old man is Luis Sandoval, right?"

"Yes, sir," Ernesto replied.

The man laughed in a sneering sort of way. "I knew Luis when we were teenagers at Gompers. He was a freshman."

A pretty woman with short dark hair appeared, and Naomi introduced Ernesto to her mother, Linda. "Oh," Mrs. Martinez remarked, smiling, "I remember Luis Sandoval when we were all kids." Brutus was prowling around the room, and Linda kept looking at the dog from the corner of her eye. She led Ernesto and Naomi into the kitchen and closed the door firmly behind them.

"I know it's silly," the woman commented nervously as she put out some brownies, "but I hate that dog."

Ernesto was surprised. He couldn't imagine his father buying a dog that Mom hated. If they were to get a dog, they'd talk it over and make sure everybody was happy with the decision.

"I don't like pit bulls myself," Ernesto responded. "I never had a bad experience with one, but we've all heard stuff . . ."

"Oh," Mrs. Martinez reacted with a shudder that seemed to shake her whole slim body. "He just terrifies me. My sons don't mind him, and Felix just adores the dog.

I guess he's okay with you, Naomi. But I'm so afraid he's going to come at me and knock me down and . . ."

"Brutus is strong all right," Naomi agreed, rolling up her sleeve. "I'd gotten his chain around my arm and he yanked it. I thought he was going to pull my arm out of its socket. It made an ugly bruise, but it's fading now."

Ernesto thought to himself, "Why would a guy get a dog that terrified of his wife? Why wouldn't she just say the dog scares me—send him back to where he came from?"

"These brownies are great," Ernesto remarked.

"Thanks," Mrs. Martinez said. "I love to bake. So, how are your parents, Ernesto? I remember Maria being such a pretty girl and nice as pie. And Luis, such a gentleman even when he was a teenager. I never knew a boy quite like him."

"They're good," Ernesto answered. "I've got two little sisters, Katalina and Juanita.

Mom stays at home and takes care of the family. She likes that."

The door opened, and Felix Martinez came into the kitchen. He grabbed two brownies and ate them quickly. For just a second, fear flashed through Mrs. Martinez's eyes. She thought the dog was with her husband.

Felix Martinez noticed her fright, and he laughed. "Can you believe this woman? She's scared stiff of a perfectly nice dog like Brutus. I grew up with dogs. I've never been afraid of a dog in my life. I prefer them to people." He turned to Ernesto. "You're scrawny, Ernie, like your father was. He was a runt. Tall, but skinny. Don't they give you enough to eat at home?"

"I eat a lot," Ernesto replied. "But my height shot up, and my weight isn't catching up yet."

"You need to eat a lot of good red meat," Mr. Martinez declared. "*Carne asada*. Refried beans. My wife there, she's a good cook. You're a great cook, Linda. You don't do much else right, but hey, the way to a guy's heart is through his stomach, right?"

Ernesto felt uncomfortable in this house. He didn't like the atmosphere. He felt sorry for Naomi, sorry that she had to live here. He thought maybe living here had made her more accepting of a jerk like Clay Aguirre.

Ernesto finished his brownie and got up. He thanked Mrs. Martinez and Naomi for asking him in. Then he walked slowly toward the door. He heard the pit bull snarling and pacing in the den, where he had been locked in. Mr. Martinez followed Ernesto. "You go in for sports, boy?"

"I've just signed up for the track team," Ernesto replied.

"That's girlie stuff," Felix Martinez growled. "I mean like football, wrestling, stuff like that. That kind of thing builds a man up. I was a linebacker in high school. I knocked guys down like they were pins in a bowling alley." He grinned at the memory.

"Yeah well," Ernesto persisted, "I love to run, and I think I'll enjoy the track team."

He didn't know what else to say. He didn't like this man—Naomi's father. Ernesto was anxious to get out of the house as quickly as possible.

"Little wimpy guys give me the creeps," Mr. Martinez declared belligerently. "You don't want to be one of them, Ernie. You want to be a real man."

Ernesto thought, "My father is more of a man than you ever were on your best day, dude. If I can be half the man he is, I'll be happy." Ernesto wished he had the courage to say that out loud, but he didn't. Maybe, he thought, he would some day. Ernesto tried to get out the door. But Mr. Martinez had more to say, and he was blocking the door.

"You afraid of playing contact sports, boy?" he challenged Ernesto.

"No sir," Ernesto replied. "I don't enjoy them as much as I enjoy track."

Mr. Martinez paid no attention to Ernesto's answer. "Because if you are, that's all the more reason to go in for that kind of sport, to get over the fear. To face your fears and conquer them—that's what life is all about. I have three boys, and they were afraid to learn to swim. So I tossed them into the water, and, boy, did they learn to swim! They were frantic, and they were mad. But they learned, you know what I'm saying? Fear is a bad thing. To conquer fear is how a man becomes a man."

Mr. Martinez was on a roll. "Boy, I got a wife who's afraid of everything. She's germ crazy. She thinks everything's dirty. She's washing here and there like the plague is coming at us. That's why I got the pit bull. I know how scared she is of mean-looking dogs. I got the biggest, meanest-looking dog I could find. And I'm gonna force her to come to terms with that. I'm getting in her face with that dog. And she's gonna get strong one way or another. I just can't stand wimpy, fearful people."

Ernesto had had a mild dislike of Felix Martinez, but now he felt hatred. He wanted to say, "Sir, I kind of despise you. Would you get your big out-of-shape body out of my way so I can leave here before I get sick over everything?" Instead, Ernesto made a polite comment. "I'm late for work. I better be going."

"Yeah, hey, see you around," Mr. Martinez said and finally moved from the door.

As Ernesto hurried down the walk, Naomi came out and caught up to him. "See you at school tomorrow, Ernie," she suggested.

"I'd call the Humane Society or something and tell them to come get the dog," Ernesto declared. "I'd do it while he was at work. That's what I'd do. I'm sorry, but I would."

Naomi's eyes widened. "Oh Ernie, he'd be so mad . . ." she whispered.

Ernesto shrugged. "It's not fair that your mom has to live like that. She shouldn't have to live in fear in her own house. That's just how I feel."

Naomi said nothing. Ernesto turned and headed for home. He had about an hour before he had to report for work, and he could get some homework done on the computer.

Ernesto now fully understood why Naomi chose a boyfriend like Clay Aguirre. He was like her father—a controlling, aggressive, kind of a mean jerk. Ernesto had read once that young people often choose boyfriends and girlfriends like their parents. He read that, if girls had abusive fathers, they would choose mean guys as boyfriends. Wanting to keep the madness going didn't make sense to him, but that's what Ernesto had read.

Maybe, Ernesto thought sadly, Naomi thought that's the way people should be: controlling guys and submissive girls.

When Ernesto got home that night after work, Mom was in the den. She was getting it ready for *Abuela* even they weren't sure she was moving in. Mom had an instinct about things. She seemed to know what was going to happen. She certainly wanted the den to be ready in case *Abuela* came.

Mom smiled at Ernesto and said, "Look honey, I got a new bedspread with geraniums on it. When your father was a boy, *Abuela* used to tell him that geraniums were like Mexicans. They thrived in harsh conditions, and they prospered."

Ernesto smiled. "It's a nice bedspread," he commented.

"And the curtains match too," Mom continued. "Look, she can just glance out the window and see the garden. I'm planting some vegetables and some flowers too. There must be flowers. There's a little stone birdbath too. *Abuela* Lena loves to watch the wild birds. It's going to be cozy, isn't it—if she comes, that is. But I think she will . . ." Mom said. "You know what, Ernie? *Abuela* loves being with the girls, and I'll have a little extra free time then to maybe write. Remember when I used to write little stories and send them in to magazines? I made a few dollars, but then

I got too busy. It would be exciting if I could start doing that again . . ."

Ernesto felt a flood of affection for his mother. She was smart, every bit as smart as his father. She had had ideas about going to college and majoring in English. But then she got married and had children, and her family came first. Even though Mom had to have some regrets that she hadn't been able to pursue her own dreams, she wasn't bitter. And now she was ready to welcome her husband's mother with such a full heart.

"It would be great if you started writing again, Mom," Ernesto urged her. "I read an essay you wrote years ago. It was in some little magazine. It was awesome."

"Oh, you're a sweetheart," Mom laughed, but she was clearly touched by the comment.

"Mom," Ernesto asked, "when you and Dad lived here before, you knew the Martinez family, right? Felix Martinez and Linda, the girl he married."

Mom paused. She got a strange look on her face. "Yes, I knew them," she replied. Ernesto could tell she had misgivings about Felix Martinez, but she wouldn't dis him. Mom didn't like to gossip. Instead she giggled and said, "Look, there's a finch in the birdbath right now!"

CHAPTER SIX

The next day, Thursday, Ernesto had permission to miss his last class at school. He had to take his driving test. And his mother drove him down to the Department of Motor Vehicles. He aced the written test, missing just one question. Then he went outside and got into the car for his test drive with the examiner. Ernesto could not remember ever being more nervous, but he had a pretty good feel for the car.

A short man, wearing glasses, appeared, giving Ernesto a thin smile. When he got in beside Ernesto, the man instructed him to pull away from the curb. Ernesto knew a kid who flunked his driving test then and there when he pulled out without looking and another car had to screech to a halt. Ernesto dutifully checked the mirrors and looked back before pulling out. He pulled slowly from the curb and entered the flow of traffic.

During the test, the examiner gave soft spoken instructions on where to turn, when to change lanes, and so on. For each instruction, Ernesto carefully looked for enough road space and gave the appropriate signals.

Ernesto was so nervous at the wheel that he worried the examiner might flunk him for that reason. He figured the guy probably thought he was a fool. "I'm pretty nervous driving right now," Ernesto explained, "because I want to be really careful."

"Don't lose that feeling," the examiner responded. His thin smile expanded into a friendlier grin. "Never feel entirely comfortable when you're driving a car. Never think you're sitting in your living room operating the remote. Driving is dangerous. Never forget that. What causes tragic accidents with most young drivers is overconfidence. Now, pull into the DMV lot and park."

As Ernesto got out of the minivan, the examiner announced, "Congratulations. You passed."

Ernesto felt as if his head was going to explode with joy. He went back into the DMV to get his picture taken and receive his temporary license. The permanent one would come later in the mail. Ernesto ran to the parking lot, where Mom was waiting by the minivan. "Mom! Mom!" he began yelling when he was about a hundred feet away. "I passed!"

Maria Sandoval laughed. Ernesto did not usually hug his mother except on special occasions. But now he took her in his arms and gave her a big hug and a kiss. She felt warm and fulfilling in his arms. Ernesto loved her so much. At this moment, he loved his father and his sisters and *Abuela* and Calico, the cat. He loved Hortencia and all his cousins and relatives and the whole world. *He had passed his driver's test.* He had joined that elite society of men and women who drove cars, who didn't need to be driven around by other people. He was a driver. Ernesto Sandoval was a driver.

Mom slid over and said, "You drive home, Ernie."

"Okay Mom," Ernesto responded eagerly. For the first time in his life, he was driving his mother!

Ernesto drove slowly and carefully. He watched people getting on buses, and he felt sorry for them. He knew that many of them preferred to ride the bus and that choosing that way of getting around was good for the environment. But still Ernesto felt sorry for them, standing there at the bus stop and waiting. He felt fortunate and privileged. He was a driver. He glanced at the drivers in the cars beside him at the traffic light. He looked at the adult men and women at the wheels, and he thought, "I'm one of you. I'm a man driving a car. I'm a motorist."

When Ernesto pulled up at the elementary school to pick up Katalina and

Juanita the girls screamed excitedly. They took turns hugging Ernesto and demanded to be taken here and there. "Did you miss any questions on that test?" Katalina wanted to know. "When I'm big enough to get my license, I won't miss one single question."

"I missed one," Ernesto admitted.

"What'd you miss?" Katalina demanded. "I bet I woulda got it."

"I said you needed to dim your lights within five hundred feet of a car you're following, but it's only three hundred feet," Ernesto answered.

"Oh," Katalina reacted, frowning.

Later, when they home with Dad, he joined in the celebration of the milestone. They drove to a nice restaurant outside the *barrio* and enjoyed chicken *enchiladas* with salad.

"You know Ernie," Dad remarked, "Dom and Carlos are already sketching out their mural on paper, deciding what it's going to look like. I talked to the principal, Ms. Sanchez, and she loved the idea. We're going to get about six kids involved, and the beauty is that most of them were taggers."

"Hey Dad, that's great," Ernesto cried.

"One other thing, though," Dad added with a quizzical look. "I'm suddenly getting a lot more respect in that American history class. It's not just because of the mural either. Carlos used to be a big problem, horsing around, talking to his friends. Now he sort of looks at me differently. I'm not just boring Mr. Sandoval anymore. I'm just curious to see if you know anything about that, Ernie?"

"You're a wonderful teacher, Luis," Mom assured him. "The kids are beginning to realize that."

"Yeah," Ernesto chimed in, concentrating on his meal. "Boy, this is one good *enchilada*."

Dad looked at Katalina and said playfully, "Do you know why they like your papa better, little one?"

"No Papa, but you're a good teacher, and they better be nice to you," Katalina declared.

"How about you, Juanita?" Dad asked. "Do you know why they respect your papa more now?"

Juanita giggled and replied, "Everybody loves you, Papa."

Now Luis Sandoval turned to Ernesto and said, "So, *mi hijo,* since nobody else has the answer, perhaps you do. Perhaps you know . . ."

"Uh, no Dad," Ernesto mumbled. "I hear good things about you all the time. This girl, Naomi, said you're an awesome teacher. She said she never liked history so much before. I'm uh . . . not surprised that so many kids like your class. You're a great teacher, Dad."

"Here's a clue maybe," Dad offered with a strange look on his face. "Carlos asked me out of a clear sky what it's like in Falluja. Now why in the world would he think I would know about Falluja?"

"Yeah?" Ernesto asked, feigning puzzlement. "That *is* strange."

"And then this girl, Luci, she wondered what an IED sounded like when it went off," Luis Sandoval went on.

"No kidding?" Ernesto said, finding it harder to get absorbed in his chicken *enchilada*. Finally he looked up and met his father's gaze. "I guess I might have said something real fast, just in passing, you know. I might have let something slip . . ."

"There's nothing wrong in them knowing you served your country, Luis," Maria Sandoval suggested. "You took two years out of your life—*our lives*—and served your country under terrible circumstances."

"I don't trade on that, though," Dad protested.

"I'm telling you," Ernesto tried to change the subject. "I never tasted such good *enchiladas*. And the *salsa!* I just want to keep on dipping into the *salsa*. Oh, by the way, I'm on the track team now. Did I tell you that, Dad?"

"Yes, you did," Dad responded. "Gus Muñoz is really excited. He told me you're the best prospect he's seen in ages. The poor kids on the team now are pretty slow. He's pinning all his hopes on you."

"I'm gonna try not to disappoint him," Ernesto promised, glad that they had moved away from the subject of Falluja and IEDs.

The following Tuesday, when Ernesto met the team for the first time, he didn't recognize any of the other boys, except for Julio Avila who was in his math class and who was also new to the team. Julio looked as though he might be fast too. He figured Ernesto to be a potential rival. Julio figured he'd be the star of the team. Now he wasn't so sure. Eddie Gonzales and Jorge Aguilar had been on the team for a while, and they were improving very slowly.

"We're gonna see what you guys got in the hundred meter," Gus Muñoz announced. "I want you to give it your best."

CHAPTER SIX

Ernesto stood at the starting line with the other three boys. Now he was going to see whether all the practice running he had done would pay off.

"Get set—go!" Muñoz shouted, and the boys took off.

Julio Avila was out front early on, and Ernesto was right behind him. Jorge and Eddie were lagging as usual, but they were doing a little better than they usually did.

At the halfway mark, Ernesto took the lead from Julio and finished the race about three yards ahead of him. The disappointment was raw on Julio's face. He had expected to win.

"Ernie, Julio, you were good," Coach Muñoz announced. "Eddie, you were better, and, Jorge, you got your work cut out for you. All you guys, practice, practice. Run all you can. You'll get stronger and faster."

After the practice, when Ernesto was back in his T-shirt and jeans, Julio came over. "Hey big shot, where did you come from anyway?" he asked.

"I'm a homeboy, but we've been away for about ten years," Ernesto replied. "I was born here in the *barrio,* but Dad got a job teaching up in LA. So we moved away."

"Coach said your name was Sandoval," Julio mentioned. "You Luis Sandoval's kid?"

"Yeah," Ernesto replied, stiffening for what he thought might come next. Julio didn't like him because he was a rival. What better way to hurt Ernesto than to dis his father?

"He's a pretty good teacher," Julio offered. "He knows his stuff. The other day some wiseguy tried to trip him up on California history, and he came right back with the goods. I'm liking the class. But listen up, dude." Julio's manner changed. "I'm gonna be the star of this team. You're not ever beating me again like you did today. I'm gonna burn up the track, man. I've been running my tail off, dude. I'm gonna beat you like a rug."

"We're both giving it our best shots, dude," Ernesto came back. "May the best guy win." Ernesto held out his hand, but Julio didn't take it.

"You know something, Sandoval?" Julio said. "I got a good reason to make it big in track. I got busted last year. It looked like I wasn't even gonna come back for my junior year. My old man just about gave up on me, and he ain't got much else keepin' him going. Rips my gut how I disappointed him. I made some big mistakes, but I'm gonna shine on the track. Nobody gonna take that away from me."

Julio's voice was an angry snarl. "You got a cool old man, and you probably come from a great family. I got no mom, and my old man is a bitter loser. He never got the breaks. He ain't never had nothin' to be proud of. My old man ain't the best in the world, that's for sure. But he didn't deserve the kind of life he's been handed, okay?"

"I hear you," Ernesto responded softly. "And I got a lot of respect for where you're coming from." Ernesto wasn't angry at the boy for his blunt fury. He understood.

Ernesto *did* have a good family. His family was a gift that a lot of kids at Cesar Chavez High School and other places didn't have. Ernesto didn't spend a lot of time trying to figure out why things happened as they did. But he knew one thing. A lot of people were dealt an awful hand, and you needed to cut them some slack for that.

As Ernesto headed for home, he knew he wouldn't slow down just to let Julio Avila win. That would be cheating and letting the team down. and he'd have no part of that. Ernesto would do his best. He was just hoping that they'd have a relay race and that he and Julio could work together to bring the team to victory. He was looking forward to handing the baton to Julio and seeing the team win. That would be a very good thing.

"Ernie," Naomi Martinez called to him as he walked from the campus.

Ernesto turned. She wore a red pullover and jeans, and her dark hair was pulled back in a ponytail. She looked beautiful, but a terrible sadness was in her eyes as she drew near. "He won't even talk to me," she said in a leaden voice. "I've said I was sorry a dozen times, and he won't even talk to me."

Ernesto wanted to tell her that Clay Aguirre was a creep and that, if he'd broken up with Naomi, it was the best day of her life. But he knew that wasn't what she wanted or even needed to hear. She was too raw, too vulnerable right now to deal with that possibility head-on.

"Ernie," she continued, "you got time to just hang with me for a while?"

"Yeah, sure," Ernesto agreed. The thought of hanging out with Naomi was so appealing that ordinarily his spirits would have soared. But now she was looking for a shoulder to cry on. That's all she needed, and he knew it. But he was willing to offer whatever she needed. "We can go over to Hortencia's and get a little table in the back," he suggested. "There won't be many people there now. Hortencia doesn't mind how long people stay when business is slow . . ."

"Okay," Naomi agreed gratefully and walked beside Ernesto toward Hortencia's. Ernesto wondered what Clay Aguirre would do if he saw them walking together. Clay probably thought he still owned Naomi. He was giving her the silent treatment to punish her for not coming through on the school report. But a creep like Clay probably expected her to wait patiently and alone until he was good and ready to resume the relationship.

Ernesto didn't know exactly how to handle his situation. Could he console her by saying Clay Aguirre would soon come to his senses and apologize for his ugly behavior? The words would only stick in Ernesto's throat. In the first place, he hated the idea of Naomi being with Aguirre again. In the second place, he wanted her so much himself that he couldn't fake a hope that Aguirre would forgive and forget.

They found a quiet little table, and Hortencia brought coffee. "I just need to be with someone nice for a little while," Naomi explained, pouring a lot of sugar in her coffee. Her hands trembled. Her soft, mocha-colored little hands trembled. Ernesto saw them and wanted to kill Clay Aguirre.

"You okay, Naomi?" he asked her.

"Yeah, I'm okay," she assured him. "It's just that he's never been so mean before. We've had problems, and we usually get them squared away in a day or so. But now! I guess it's because he's struggling so hard to stay on the football team. I know he's under a lot of pressure. The team sort of depends on him. I understand that. If he gets below a C in English, it could sink him. Oh Ernie, how could I have been so stupid to leave that report lying there on the computer table? Oh Ernie, I shouldn't be bothering you with my problems, but there's really nobody I can talk to. Mom is so stressed out, and my brothers couldn't care less."

"No, it's okay," Ernesto assured her. "I'm glad to help any way I can. . . . Uh, would you resent some straight talk, Naomi?"

Naomi smiled ruefully. "I know what you're thinking. Clay is a jerk, and why am I bothering with him? Ernie, *I love him*. I've loved him since middle school . . . and he *can* be nice. Really he can. I know if it wasn't for him being so stressed about his football eligibility, he wouldn't be acting like that."

"Well," Ernesto offered, "I'm here for you if you need me."

"You're a cool guy," Naomi told him.

"Naomi," Ernesto protested, "I'm nothing special. I just got my driver's license. So if you'd want to go someplace when I get a car . . . I mean, just give me a call." Ernesto regretted his words the minute they left his mouth. He thought she had to be shocked that he'd even hint at dating her. "I'm no big deal," he said hurriedly, "but, you know, if you—"

"You *are* a big deal, Ernie," Naomi insisted. "Don't put yourself down. You're smart and good-looking. Most of all, you're a very good person."

Ernesto felt the room swirl around him. The advertisements for *enchiladas* on the wall, the red and green signs offering *menudo, pozole, tortas cubanas*—all of it ran past him in a colorful river. Could he be making a tiny inroad into Naomi's heart? Did she really see such good qualities in him? Did he have a chance? The possibilities, however remote, made his head spin.

"Well Ernie, thanks for letting me vent," Naomi concluded. "I guess I'll go home now. Mom is probably hiding in the kitchen with Brutus snarling at the door. She needs me to be there so I can get him into the den."

"We can walk home together," Ernesto suggested as they got up from the table.

As they walked, Ernesto asked, "Aren't you afraid of the pit bull, Naomi?"

"No," Naomi said decisively. "He's not bad deep down. I know he's a good dog. He just doesn't know his own strength. I guess he's like Clay sometimes. He's mean and snarly, but he's not really dangerous."

Ernesto remembered the look on Clay Aguirre's face when he retrieved the papers Naomi had dropped. He looked mean enough to punch Ernesto's lights out. Ernesto was not sure whether Clay or the pit bull wasn't dangerous. But if he had even a small chance of getting something going with Naomi, Ernesto was not going to be scared away.

When Ernesto got home, he called Abel. "You won't believe this, man," he told his friend, "but Naomi wanted to go someplace and talk to me. We ended up at Hortencia's. Naomi was real nice. She's really hurt by how that jerk Aguirre is treating her, but she said some nice things about me, man. It like blew my mind, I swear."

"Watch yourself, dude" Abel cautioned. "She might be trying to play you for a fool. If Aguirre thinks you're moving in on her, she thinks she'll make him jealous and then he's gonna make up with her. Chicks do that sometimes."

"She's not that kind of a girl, Abel," Ernesto protested. "She's not gaming me. I could tell. She's really hurting over this thing with Aguirre. But I could see it in her eyes that maybe she likes me a little bit . . . No bull man. I could see it!"

CHAPTER SEVEN

Ernesto dropped his shirt in the bathroom and looked at himself in the mirror. He thought he was too skinny. He needed to bulk up, do weights or something. He didn't like Naomi's father, but the guy had a point. Ernesto didn't want to be a little wimpy guy. Naomi was attracted to something about Ernesto Sandoval, and he needed to build on that. Chicks liked guys who were ripped, Ernesto figured.

Ernesto dug in his closet for the weights he used to play around with. He never took bodybuilding seriously, but now he was interested in building some muscle. He wanted to be one of those dudes who put on a T-shirt and could show some muscles underneath it. When Ernesto put on a T-shirt, it hung on him like a sack.

Ernesto was feeling good, unusually good. Everything seemed to be going his way. He had some friends at Cesar Chavez High School now, and he felt more at home. A lot of kids said "Hi" when he came by. He didn't feel like such a stranger anymore. And he was remembering Naomi's kind words and placing a lot of hope in them. He knew it would take time, but at least he knew she liked him.

Ernesto went online to do a paper for Mr. Escalante's science class. He was well into it when he heard his father come home from work. Usually he and Mom had a cup of coffee right away so that they could talk about their day. This time Dad went right to the kitchen, and Ernesto overheard his parents speaking in serious voices. An alarm went off in Ernesto's brain. Something important had happened. Maybe something bad. Maybe trouble at school. Ernesto shared a bad habit with his father: He usually expected the worst. Now he didn't like the sound of his parents' voices. Usually they laughed together. Not now.

Ernesto did not want to eavesdrop, but he had to know what they were talking about. He hurried into the hallway and listened to the voices from the kitchen.

"I saw the doctor this morning," Mom advised her husband.

"You didn't tell me you were seeing the doctor today," Dad exclaimed. "What's the matter, Maria?"

"I didn't want to bother you when it was probably just nothing," Mom explained. "You've got enough on your plate, Luis. Luis! Don't look so worried. Everything is all right. Everything is fine."

"What did you go to the doctor for?" Dad asked, still sounding worried. "Maria, I want you to share such things with me. It is never a bother to me. You must understand that."

"I thought I was pregnant, Luis," Ernesto's mother stated. "I had a feeling, but then I thought, no, not now, not after six years since Juanita. I was sure Juanita was the last, but you know how we always wanted four? How we would talk about babies and we said, *uno, dos, tres, cuatro*. And then we'd say, '*Basta,* enough!' " Mom laughed then and announced, "Luis, *cuatro* is coming!"

"Maria, no! Are you kidding me?" Dad's voice sounded strange. Ernesto couldn't figure out his mood. "A baby is coming, Maria?"

"I am pregnant, Luis," Mom affirmed. "The doctor told me today."

Their voices stopped then. Ernesto knew that Dad had taken Mom in his arms and that they were hugging each other. When they drew apart, Mom said, "You are happy aren't you?"

"Yes, I'm happy," Dad declared. "I am very happy. But Maria, do you still think my mama should—"

"Even more so now," Mom insisted. "She will be a wonderful help just being here with the girls."

"Maria, are you sure you feel well?" Dad asked.

"I have never felt better, Luis," Mom assured Dad. "I always feel very good when I'm expecting a baby. I feel on top of the world, Luis. *Abuela* can play games with the girls while I am tending the baby. It's what we always wanted. Oh Luis, *cuatro* is coming at last!"

They laughed then.

It was wonderful, exciting news, but Ernesto knew it meant more responsibility for his father. Four children now. Keeping his job was even more important than ever. It was even more crucial that they liked him at Cesar Chavez High School and would ask him back next year. Ernesto understood how his father's mind worked because it was close to how Ernesto's worked. Worries tended to fly through and darken the sky. What-ifs showed up to haunt him. What if he was not asked back next year? What if he couldn't find another position? Ernesto knew that his father was genuinely happy about the baby, but still he would worry more now. Mom lived in a sunny, unclouded world, confident that all would be well. She didn't worry much. But Dad rarely saw an unclouded blue sky. Always he looked for small clouds on the horizon, threatening to darken, grow bigger, and eventually obscure the sun itself.

Ernesto withdrew to his room. When his parents brought him the news, he wouldn't admit that he'd been listening and he already knew. Mom would probably be the one to tell him. Ernesto made up his mind to act properly surprised. He felt a little guilty that he'd already discovered the secret before he was told. But he couldn't help himself. When he heard them talking, he had thought the worst, as usual.

Ernesto sat down to ponder the new development. He was eight when Katalina was born. She was tiny and cute, and she delighted him. But he had been afraid to touch her lest she would break. Ernesto was ten when Juanita was born, and he was more confident. He knew she wouldn't break easily. It was fun helping Mom take care of her.

But now Ernesto was sixteen, and another baby was coming. He didn't know how he felt about that prospect. Ernesto was almost a man. Up in Los Angeles, he had a friend named Hector who became a father at sixteen. His girlfriend was fifteen. The girl took her baby home from the hospital to her parents. By that time, Hector had dropped out of school and run from his problems. Ernesto never saw him again. Ernesto wondered sometimes whether Hector missed his baby or whether he thought about it at all. Ernesto could not imagine what being a young father felt like—to be so young, not even to have graduated high school, not to have a real job. Ernesto felt sorry for Hector and for the girl and for the baby too. Ernesto thought his new baby brother or sister was very lucky to have parents like Mom and Dad. The baby would never lack for love. That was a big thing.

Ernesto would love the new baby too, as he loved his sisters. He would try to be a good example to the child, even though he was so much older.

Mom knocked on Ernesto's bedroom door.

"You busy, Ernie?" she asked.

"Come on in, Mom," Ernesto said.

"Ernie, I just told your father some big news," Mom began. "Now I'm telling you. We're going to have a baby. In about six months." Mom had a funny look on her face. She giggled. "You were listening, weren't you? You already know."

"I'm sorry, Mom," Ernesto apologized. "I heard you and Dad talking seriously, and I was worried that something was wrong."

Mom walked closer to her son and gave him a playful poke. "You are your father's son. A worry wart. Always expecting the worst. We have to trust, *mi niño*. We have to trust. I am very happy. I think it will be a boy. I just feel it. We will have our dream. Two boys and two girls."

Ernesto gave his mother a hug. "I'm happy for you and Dad, Mom," he said.

"I'm going to tell the girls now," Mom announced and left the room.

Less than a minute later, Ernesto heard happy screams coming from the living room. Katalina was excited, but Juanita was ballistic. In a few seconds, both girls raced into Ernesto's room.

"Mama's gonna have a baby, Ernie!" Juanita screamed, leaping onto Ernesto's bed and jumping up and down. "I'm gonna help take care of the baby. Maybe I won't go to school when the baby is small, 'cause I want to take care of it every single day."

"Mama and Papa won't let you stay home from school Juanita," Katalina protested sternly. "*Abuela* will be here to help Mama. You don't want to be *estupida,* Juanita, like those *bobos* who stop going to school. I think the new baby will be a girl, and we must be good examples to our little sister."

Ernesto smiled to himself. He loved both his sisters dearly. Juanita was more like Mom, a free spirit, all sunshine and hope. Katalina was more like Ernesto and Dad. She was looking for the clouds. She was starting to realize there were pitfalls out there. You had to avoid making the wrong choices. Even if you did everything right, things didn't always turn out right.

How quickly their joy changed to sadness that night was astonishing. The Sandoval family went from celebrating the news of Mom's pregnancy to shock and sorrow. One minute they were still sitting around the dining room table, having eaten *filete de cerdo* and bantering about little things. The girls had been packed off to bed.

Then, around eight-thirty, the phone rang. Mom answered the phone and listened for a minute, her smile slowly fading. Then the look on her face turned stark. Hortencia was calling. After Mom hung up the phone, she looked stunned as she related what Hortencia had told her family.

"That was Hortencia," Mom reported to her son and husband. "She said there was a birthday party on her street. She had heard singing and laughter. A girl was turning sixteen, and all her friends were there. Then shots were fired, and screams replaced the laughter. Hortencia saw police cars and an ambulance. It was chaos, as the kids spilled into the street. A boy had been shot. He hadn't been at the party for long. Another boy, who had not been invited to the party, followed him, and the shooting took place in the driveway of the house. Hortencia doesn't know the name of the boy who was shot. She doesn't know if he . . ." Mom couldn't finish.

Luis Sandoval wondered immediately whether the shooter or the victim was in his classes at Chavez High. Ernesto wondered whether either boy was one of his new friends.

Hortencia called again. The boy who was shot was Tommy Alvarado. He had been Hortencia's paperboy when he was twelve. He was such a nice, polite boy, she said. Hortencia did not know the name of the shooter, but he was in police custody.

When Mom put down the phone, Ernesto commented, "I don't know him. Not by name anyway. I might have seen him, but I don't recognize the name."

Luis Sandoval briefly put his face in his hands. "*Dios mío!*" he moaned.

"You know him, Luis?" Mom asked gently.

"American history, second period," he sighed. "Always smiling. A good kid. Asks interesting questions. He listens. They don't all listen. Good grades too. He wants . . . he *wants* to go into the Marines—fly a chopper—then maybe be an archeologist. Did my sister say how bad it is?"

"Hortencia didn't know," Mom answered. "He was still alive when they took him away, but it looked . . . you know . . . bad."

Ernesto found it hard to swallow all of a sudden. He had no saliva in his mouth. Maybe Tommy Alvarado was in one of his classes. Maybe when he saw his picture, he would recognize him. Maybe the two boys had shared a joke about how stale the doughnuts were in the vending machine. Maybe they had discussed the Chargers' chances this year.

"My God!" Luis Sandoval cried. "What could be so bad that they shoot each other when they are only children?"

A shooting had occurred at the school in Los Angeles too. A girl coming from a party was caught in the crossfire between two warring groups of gangbangers. Ernesto didn't know her well, but she was in one of his classes. Her name was Britney. Ernesto remembered the little shrine that sprung up immediately at the spot where Britney died. Candles in glass jars with the image of Our Lady of Guadalupe on them, flowers, teddy bears, pictures of the girl smiling. Ernesto remembered thinking who would shoot a girl like that? But the answer was that no one was even aiming at her. She was an innocent casualty, and war brings a lot of innocent casualties. Her death was sad and insane. Britney was just seventeen. She had lived only one year longer than Ernesto had already lived.

"Hortencia said her neighbor told her that the argument was over a girl," Mom explained. "The girl had just broken up with her boyfriend, and he was the shooter. He came to the party to shoot the new boyfriend. That's what Hortencia's neighbor said anyway. Maybe it's true, and maybe it's not."

They did not learn until morning, as they ate their breakfast, that Tommy Alvarado had died. The news report didn't give the shooter's name because he was only sixteen, but it was said that he had gang connections and was a high school dropout.

At the breakfast table, Mom gently explained to Katalina and Juanita why everyone was so sad. "Last night," she began, "*Tía* Hortencia called. A boy your daddy teaches in class died last night, and we feel really bad."

"How come he died?" Juanita asked.

"He was shot by another boy," Dad answered. He wasn't going to sugarcoat the answer, not even to an eight-year-old and a six-year-old. Soon—too soon—his little girls would be going out into the world where such things happen. They needed to know. "The two boys were fighting over a girl, it seems. The boy who did the shooting had lost the girl, and he was mad at the boy she was going with now. So he shot him."

The girls grew quiet, even Juanita. Ernesto thought it would be very hard for his father to look at the desk where Tommy Alvarado usually sat and to know he would not sit there ever again. If a student had a disease for a long time and you knew what was coming, you could prepare yourself. But Tommy was in his place yesterday, looking up intently as Dad lectured.

Ernesto thought he had it easier than his dad. He couldn't place the boy, and he really didn't want to. Abel had lent Ernesto his copy of last year's yearbook, figuring it would help Ernesto know who was who.

Tommy Alvarado was a sophomore last year. His face would have been there among the others. Ernesto could have checked out the yearbook, but he didn't.

After breakfast, Abel came by the house as usual to walk to school with Ernesto. He talked about the shooting right away. Unlike Ernesto, he knew the boy. "What a bummer," he lamented bitterly. "Tommy didn't have that coming. He was a good guy."

"You close to the guy?" Ernesto asked.

"We weren't close pals or anything," Abel answered, "But we knew each other since middle school. He was a good guy, Ernie. I'm sure you've seen him. He was in Ms. Hunt's English class with us. He was a big Chargers fan. Kind of a medium-sized guy. His nose was a little crooked. He broke it when he fell out of a tree couple years ago, and his parents were saving up the money to get it fixed."

Ernesto closed his eyes. Sadly, he remembered Tommy's face. When they were talking about Lady Macbeth, he seemed very intent. He sat in the third row, right behind Naomi. One day both Ernesto and Tommy Alvarado were looking at the girl. She had on an amazing pair of jeans with a little glittery puma stitched on the back pocket. Ernesto remembered him and Tommy grinning at each other.

Ernesto took a long, deep breath. He wondered who the girl was that they fought over. He wondered what she felt. One boy was dead, and another was facing murder charges—all over her. Ernesto thought she must feel terrible, even though it probably wasn't her fault. If she was a tease and she played the boys against each other, then Ernesto figured she ought to feel guilty like Lady Macbeth did. It should haunt her. But maybe she was a nice girl who finally got away from a bad dude, and then something terrible and unexpected happened.

Ernesto thought about Naomi Martinez. A lot of guys looked at her. She was beautiful. Sometimes a chick just can't help being beautiful. Maybe the girl the two boys fought over was beautiful like Naomi. Maybe the shooter was a creep like Clay Aguirre. But Ernesto quickly told himself that Aguirre would never get violent like that.

"Hey man," Abel remarked, "you look sick."

"I was just thinking about that poor dead guy," Ernesto replied.

They were getting close to Cesar Chavez High School. They could see the mural with Chavez's gentle, kindly smile. Ernesto loved that mural. It was the first thing he saw at Chavez High that he liked, the lovely painting of a good, decent, peaceful man who tried so hard to make life better for poor people. "I just hate it when stuff like that shooting happens. It's so stupid, so useless . . . ," Ernesto added.

"You know what, man?" Abel offered. "You be careful messing with Naomi, you understand? Guys go berserk when they think they're losing their chick."

"Abel," Ernesto insisted, "Clay Aguirre is a jerk, but he's no criminal gangbanger."

"Listen to me, man," Abel persisted. "You know the biggest reason why chicks get killed? I mean girlfriends and even wives. It's another guy moving in. Listen to what I'm saying."

CHAPTER EIGHT

Then Ernesto saw Naomi Martinez, standing by the mural of Cesar Chavez. She looked terribly upset.

"Hey Naomi, you okay?" Ernesto asked, hurrying toward the girl. Abel shrugged his shoulders and walked on to his first class.

"Yeah," Naomi replied. "My parents had a big fight this morning. Mom almost never has the guts to fight back, but this morning she just blew up like a crazy lady. She said she just knew Brutus was going to rip her face off. She just knew it. She says she's not going to stay in the house unless the dog goes, and Dad stood his ground. He called her a coward and said he was ashamed of her. He said Brutus was the sweetest dog in the whole *barrio*. If Mom gave the dog half a chance, she'd like him too. I swear, Ernie, I think Mom has blown a gasket or something. I've *never* seen her yelling at Dad like that. I think the pit bull just pushed her over the edge, but I'm so scared they'll split up or something!"

"I don't blame your Mom," Ernesto responded. "It's her house too. She has the right to feel safe in her own home. I mean, yeah, maybe the dog is okay and all that. But if she's feeling that bad about it, the dog should go."

"But Dad would never get rid of the dog," Naomi insisted, fear in her face. "I think he'd let Mom go first."

"It'll blow over, Naomi," Ernesto assured her. "Married people fight like that, and it mostly blows over. Even my parents had one big fight that scared the daylights out of me."

Naomi's eyes widened. "*Your dad*? He seems so calm and cool," she exclaimed.

"Well, it was mostly Mom," Ernesto explained. He could smile about it now. But at the time he was almost as scared as Naomi that his parents were breaking up. Ernesto was only twelve, and he overheard Mom yelling in his parents' bedroom. He was totally shocked.

"Luis!" Mom shouted. "You have three children! Juanita is just a baby! How can you even consider deploying with your unit to Iraq? I mean, the school would get you a deferment." Her voice quivered with emotion.

"Most of the other guys are in the same boat," Dad argued. "We're mostly family men in the Guard. Maria, you were okay with it when I joined the National Guard. We discussed it."

"Luis," Mom objected, "I had no idea it would mean going to Iraq and fighting in a war. I thought the National Guard put out riots in the United States. I thought they did jobs at home."

In the end, Luis Sandoval deployed to Iraq with his unit, and for two years Mom supported him. She called him and sent him packages. When he came home at last, no wife ran faster to greet her returning soldier, no wife flung herself into a man's arms with more fervor.

"Who won that big argument in your house?" Naomi asked.

"Dad did," Ernesto replied, "and Mom was a good sport about it in the end."

"I think my father is going to win this argument too," Naomi concluded. "He was so mad this morning that for a minute I thought he was going to . . . " she paused. "He never has actually hit Mom, but he's shoved her a few times."

Ernesto said nothing but nodded his head slightly. It was if he were saying, "I figured as much."

Ernesto and Naomi walked toward English class. She had heard about Tommy Alvarado getting killed last night. "I talked to Tommy once or twice," she remarked. "He seemed pretty nice. I knew he'd started dating some girl over on Greenleaf. He was really excited about that. Tommy never had a serious girlfriend before. I don't know anything about the girl except she didn't go to school here. I think she dropped out of some other high school. The guy who killed Tommy, he was a gangbanger, they said. The girl, I guess she was his chick. Then Tommy came along, and the girl saw what a really nice guy was like and she dropped the creep."

"Tommy was in my father's history class," Ernesto said. "Dad liked the kid. He feels really bad about what happened."

Ernesto then thought about his plans to look for a car this weekend or next. He wondered whether Naomi would like to go with him. It wouldn't be a date or anything like that. But, since she was on the outs with Clay Aguirre, maybe she'd like to hang with Ernesto and help him find a car. Ernesto worked up the courage to ask her by the time they were almost at English. "Uh, Naomi, I'm going to look at a car maybe this weekend. Do you want to help check it out?" he asked. "We could get something to eat later. I was looking on the

Internet, and I found a car I could afford. The seller said it runs great."

Naomi didn't answer him right away about going with him. "What kind of a car is it?" she asked.

"Well, it's not the kind of car I want," Ernesto admitted, "but it's only five hundred dollars, and I can handle that. I'd just drive it for a short time until I got more money. Then I'd trade it in on something I liked. It's uh . . . a Volvo."

"A Volvo!" Naomi laughed. "My grandma has a Volvo!"

"Yeah, I hear you," he chuckled. "But, like I said, it's supposed to run good, and I could use it until I had more money. I'm really anxious for wheels, Naomi. I'm going to borrow my parents' car on Sunday and go take a look at the Volvo. If you got nothing better to do, you could maybe come along."

"Thanks, Ernie. But, you know," Naomi responded. "Clay texted me last night. It turns out he's not going to flunk English after all because of my bad. I think he wants to make up."

"Hey stick man!" came a sharp voice behind Ernesto. "You still trying to make time with my chick?" Ernesto turned to see a glowering Clay Aguirre.

"Ernie was just asking me about a car he's interested in buying, Clay," Naomi explained, looking embarrassed.

"Get lost, stick man," Clay snarled.

"Clay," Naomi intervened, "Ernie can get a Volvo for five hundred dollars." Ernesto wished she hadn't mentioned that he was looking into buying a Volvo.

Clay Aguirre laughed. "Now why doesn't it surprise me that this jerk wants to buy a Volvo?" he crowed.

Ernesto had the horrible feeling that they were both laughing at him, Naomi and Aguirre. When Naomi was having a hard time with Aguirre, she was sweet and vulnerable. Now that they'd patched up their quarrel, she was securely in his camp again. She was a different person.

Just now Ernesto did not like Naomi Martinez. He felt like her mother felt about the pit bull.

"We can go to that club I told you about, babe," Clay was telling Naomi. "I found this cool band on Facebook, and they're performing. They're real edgy."

"Sounds good!" Naomi exclaimed.

Now in the classroom, Ernesto quickly sat down and made up his mind. He wouldn't spend so much time daydreaming about Naomi Martinez anymore. After class, Ernesto texted Gabriella: "FWIW. No fun around here. Trying track. MU."

"Busy, busy, here," Gabriella texted back. "GTG." She had to go. No surprise there. Gabriella was doing much better without Ernesto than he was doing without her. She probably had a new boyfriend already. Why not? She was cute. She knew Ernesto wasn't coming back.

Ernesto took a shortcut behind the science building on his way to speech. Suddenly, somebody was behind him.

"Hey stick man, we gotta talk," Clay Aguirre demanded.

Ernesto turned. "What's up?" he said, trying to sound casual. He couldn't imagine what Aguirre wanted with him. Obviously, Naomi and Clay were hot and heavy again.

"You're getting in my craw, man," Clay declared, getting close to Ernesto. "When me and Naomi had that little misunderstanding, you moved right in. You struck like a snake. My friends told me you and her were over at Hortencia's, sitting way in the back holding hands."

"That's a lie," Ernesto objected. "That never happened, man."

"Yeah? That ain't what I hear," Clay snarled in a menacing voice. "I heard you were all over her."

Ernesto glanced around. The spot was secluded. Most of the students and teachers were in classrooms. If Clay tried to pull something, Ernesto would have a problem. Clay Aguirre had more than fifty pounds on Ernesto. He could do a lot of damage.

"Naomi, she's kind of a romantic chick," Clay insisted. "She thinks it's gotta be violins all the time. But when I got a problem with a chick, I'm gonna let her know it. You're a weak, wimpy dude. Sometimes, to a weak-minded chick, that kinda guy looks appealing, especially when her man has gotten tough with her. I'm just tellin' you man, stop being there when me and Naomi got problems. Stop tryin' to grab her when she stumbles. Don't move in on my chick, man. I'm warnin' you."

"I wasn't moving in," Ernesto replied.

"You got the hots for her, man," Clay snarled. "Don't lie about it." Clay took a step closer. "You make trouble for me with Naomi, and I'll beat you up so bad even your own Mama won't recognize you."

"You're crazy, dude," Ernesto told him.

For the first time in his life, Ernesto desperately wanted to be strong and tough and able to take on somebody like Clay Aguirre, man to man. He resolved to exercise and to do whatever it took to get strong—strong enough to whip Aguirre. He didn't want to be standing like this anymore, afraid of the loudmouthed punk facing him.

Clay moved quickly, grabbing Ernesto's shirt front. He pushed him hard against the stucco wall of the science building, yelling in his face, "Maybe you don't like the shape of your nose, Sandoval," he seethed. "Maybe you'd like a couple slits in your lip. Maybe you're tired of having so many teeth in your mouth. I can fix all that, Sandoval, you get my meaning? Naomi, she belongs to me. She's mine. No matter what happens between us, she's mine."

He tightened his grip on Ernesto's shirt front, banging his head back against the stucco wall. He didn't do it hard enough to cause damage. But he let Ernesto know he could have if he wanted. Then he sneered and released Ernesto. "Listen, man, there's plenty ugly chicks around Chavez High for guys like you. You find yourself a dog, man. They'd go for a loser like you."

With that, Clay strode off, his muscles straining at his tight T-shirt. Ernesto felt a rage he had never experienced before. He had run into a few bullies up in Los Angeles, but he'd never been humiliated like this. Ernesto was so angry he felt sick to his stomach. He didn't want to sit in speech class and learn how to make a speech entertaining. He didn't want to sit in any class just now. But he forced himself to go to class. He wasn't going to let Clay Aguirre win in any way. Messing Ernesto up academically would suit Aguirre fine. And Ernesto was not going to let that happen.

When Ernesto got home that night after work, he started lifting weights.

"Whatcha doing?" Juanita asked.

"Building muscles, Juanita," Ernesto explained. "Getting strong."

"You wanna be like the Incredible Hulk?" Juanita giggled. She'd just seen the old movie on TV.

"Yeah," Ernesto replied.

"You wanna be green like him too?" Juanita asked, giggling more.

"Maybe," Ernesto answered. "Just so I'm big and tough. I don't want no creeps bullying me and getting away with it."

Luis Sandoval heard that, and he stopped. "Somebody at school giving you a hard time, Ernie?" he inquired.

"No Dad," Ernesto lied. "I'm just sick of being skinny."

Luis Sandoval was an intuitive man. He knew his children pretty well. "Because if you are being bullied at school, Ernie, fighting isn't the solution. The bully has got to be exposed and dealt with."

"Yeah, right," Ernesto thought to himself. "I should go whining to Ms. Sanchez about Clay Aguirre being mean to me. That'd make me oh so popular at school. Whiny, wimpy Ernesto Sandoval is making trouble for the best football player on the team. Then I'd have *all* Clay's buddies mad at me."

Ernesto looked at his father. He was a handsome man—young-looking, trim. He had always been underweight, but not like Ernesto. Now in his late thirties, he'd added enough weight to look good. "You were skinny like me in high school, huh Dad?" Ernesto asked.

"Yep," Dad admitted. "And all the pretty girls went for the guys with big thick necks. Most of those poor jerks ended up in dead-end jobs because they thought they had it made just being jocks. Only trouble is very few high school stars make the cut for pro-football jobs in the real world. I was the skinny nerd with glasses, and I snagged the prettiest girl at school and a profession."

Ernesto smiled. "Dad, I just want to be ripped, you know? It would make me feel better."

"Who's the special girl you're trying to impress, Ernie?" Dad asked with a twinkle in his eye.

"Well no . . . ," Ernesto objected. "But there is one girl in my class . . . Naomi Martinez. She's something else."

"Yes, she's in my American history class." Dad knew her. "Smart, nice girl. Very lovely too." He was too professional to say more. He was too honorable to reach back into his own youth and talk about his troubles with Felix Martinez, Naomi's father.

The next day, Saturday, some students and teachers from Cesar Chavez High School attended the funeral for Tommy Alvarado. It was held at Our Lady of Guadalupe Church at three in the afternoon. Ernesto didn't know Tommy, but Tommy had been in his father's class. So Ernesto went with his father. Tommy Alvarado was a member of the junior class and so was Ernesto. That was another reason to go.

Tommy Alvarado didn't have a great many friends. So the church wasn't packed, but the showing was respectable. Ernesto remembered the funeral for Britney, the girl who was shot in Los Angeles. At least five hundred people had attended her Mass. Many of the girl's classmates gave tearful testimonials to her excellent qualities. But here there was no such reaction. Instead of large, colorful photographs of the dead teenager at Britney's funeral, there was just Tommy's school picture. The family was a pathetic, small group—mother, grandmother, younger siblings. No one could give the eulogy. So Luis Sandoval volunteered.

"I only knew Tommy Alvarado for three weeks," Dad began. "But in that time I saw that he was a promising young man. He was curious about everything, and he was friendly and courteous. I became accustomed to looking to him to answer the tough questions, and he rarely failed me. He had an A average in my class. I could see he had a bright future, and I was delighted to be his teacher. I wept when I heard of his untimely passing. The fact that his death evoked such a strong feeling in my heart is testimony to what a fine young man he was. His death is a terrible loss to Cesar Chavez High School, to the community, and to the world he would have touched. As Tommy is taken to a better, gentler world far from the cruel violence that struck him, we have an obligation to honor his all too brief life by rejecting the mindless violence that robbed us of his presence among us. *Vaya con Dios, Tomás*."

Tommy's mother and grandmother were weeping. Ernesto was so proud of his father for delivering such a beautiful eulogy. If he hadn't stepped up to do it, nobody would have spoken on Tommy's behalf.

As Ernesto and his father walked from the church in the dying light of the day, a girl approached them. She was small-boned and lovely. She looked about thirteen, but she was older. Ernesto had never seen before, but he knew without being told that she was the girl the fight was over.

"I'm Yvette Ozono," she stated in a soft voice that sounded more like a child's than that of a young woman. "I want to thank you, sir, for the beautiful things you said about Tommy. I was afraid nobody would say nothing about him, and he was somebody. He was really special, and maybe not many people knew it. But he was. I had a boyfriend since middle school, and he was mean to me. But I didn't think I deserved no better. Then Tommy came along, and he was like an angel to me. I didn't know a boy could be so nice. He treated me with respect, you know? I fell in love with him, and he was trying to talk me into going back to school. Now I don't care about nothing. I wish I was in that box with Tommy."

Ernesto's father looked at Ernesto. Then he turned to the girl. "Yvette, let us buy you a cup of coffee," he suggested.

"No, you don't need to bother," the girl declined. "I just wanted you to know it was so good of you to give Tommy a nice send-off like that."

"Come on, Yvette," Dad insisted. "There's a little coffee shop just across the street. Let's just go over there and talk. My son here, Ernie, he was in a class with Tommy."

The three of them crossed the street and went in the coffee shop. When they were seated in a booth, Luis Sandoval spoke. "Yvette, you are a lovely young woman, and you have your whole life ahead of you. Tommy would want for you to have a good life."

"I'm the reason he's dead," Yvette sighed bitterly. "I was poison for him. I was Coyote's woman. Coyote was my boyfriend's gang name. He called me horrible names, and he pushed me around. But I knew him since I was twelve. I thought how he treated me was normal. I didn't think I deserved no better."

Yvette paused. She seemed to be running things through her mind. "Anyway," she went on, "I went and reached for something better. And that's why Tommy Alvarado had to die. I don't deserve no long life or anything. If Tommy had never met me, he'd still be alive. They wouldn't be taking him out now to put him in the ground." Tears ran down the girl's face. She was shaking.

Ernesto felt so sorry for her. She looked so young, so broken. He reached out and put his hand over hers. "It's all right," he said. "You were not to blame. Coyote did it. It wasn't your fault."

Ernesto and his father drove the girl to the apartment where she lived with her mother and several siblings. When they brought her to the door, her mother came and took the girl in her arms. The mother told the girl in Spanish over and over how much she loved her. She told Yvette that she would always love her, that she had done nothing wrong, and that she was with her family now and safe.

Luis Sandoval spoke to the mother in Spanish. He gave her his name and phone number, and he said he would help Yvette get back into school. The mother said "*Gracias señor, gracias, gracias.*"

"*Por nada, señora,*" Luis Sandoval responded before he left with Ernesto.

CHAPTER NINE

On the following Tuesday, Ernesto Sandoval went to the football field where Coach Muñoz was meeting his track team. The other boys were there too—Eddie, Jorge, Julio, along with other guys Ernesto didn't know yet.

"You guys been running?" Coach Muñoz asked. Everybody shouted out that they had.

"Okay!" Coach went on. "Now let's see who's telling me a tall tale. I can tell right away who's been running and who's been texting or checking out Facebook." A spattering of laughter followed Coach's remark.

Julio Avila ran first, and Ernesto was surprised at how fast he was. He was really running with passion. His movement looked fluid and effortless. The guy really wanted to excel, and he showed desire.

Ernesto glanced over into the bleachers, where a few students watched. He saw Carmen Ibarra and Abel. Some adults were there too, like Julio's father. Ernesto knew that the wasted-looking guy, who was about forty, had to be Julio's father. He looked listless until Julio began to run; then he stood up and cheered. That was the guy Julio was struggling to impress. Ernesto had to admire Julio for that.

Eddie and Jorge improved too, but not much. Then Ernesto's turn came up. He felt really strong. He waited at the starting line like a cougar waiting to pounce. Then, at the signal, he took off flying. He felt good. He was moving just the way he wanted to, doing everything right. By the time he circled the oval and returned to Coach Muñoz, the coach was grinning from ear to ear. "Way to go, Sandoval," he exclaimed. "Looks like we got two guys doing great."

Coach Muñoz looked at his clipboard. "You were only ten seconds behind Avila's time."

Ernesto wasn't disappointed that Julio had outrun him. Ernesto tried very hard to be the fastest, but Julio had a better reason to win. The guy over there in the stands was wearing a suit that was old when Ronald Reagan was president of the United States. But right now the old guy was pumped.

Julio Avila looked at Ernesto, wondering if Ernesto was irked that he'd come in second-best today. But Ernesto smiled and held out his hand again. This time Julio took it.

"You were awesome, man, really awesome," Ernesto congratulated him.

Julio grinned.

After they finished, Ernesto, Julio, and Julio's father, along with Carmen Ibarra, walked over to Hortencia's for *tamales*. "Hortencia made *tamales con tomatillos* today," Ernesto reported. "You guys never tasted anything like it. Yellow onions, jalapeno peppers, cilantro . . . oh man!"

On closer view, Julio's father looked even worse than he appeared in the stands. He was a smoker, and the nicotine had taken its toll on his skin. His face was deeply lined. All that was bright and alive in his face were his eyes, especially when they settled on his son. The small, black eyes reminded Ernesto of the busy, attentive eyes of a bird.

"My *muchacho,*" Mr. Avila declared. "He's something, eh? Like the wind goes, eh Julio?"

Julio grinned. "I just got started, Papa. You ain't seen nothin' yet," he promised. "I'm runnin' every chance I get. I'm runnin' in my sleep!" Everybody at the table laughed. Ernesto knew Julio was his biggest rival, but he liked him. He thought one day they could be friends. He was almost sure of it. No matter who ended up running faster, they could be friends.

"Know what, Julio?" Carmen announced. "I don't have a boyfriend, and Ernie doesn't have a girlfriend. So we agreed to be make believe we're boyfriend and girlfriend for each other."

"Cool," Julio responded.

"You guys, I'm having a party at my house," Carmen went on. "A real blast. You've never seen anything like parties at my house. You guys are invited—Ernie, Julio. I live on Nuthatch Lane. Papa said it fits us. The Ibarras are nuts, he says. And it's true too. My father makes sure everything is cool at the party, that no gangbangers or booze hounds show up. Papa's like a sheriff. He's not really a sheriff. But he wears a plastic badge he got in a cereal box. He'll arrest you if you're out of line and lock you in the tool shed. His name is Emilio Zapata Ibarra. If the devil himself showed up at the party, Papa would scare him off."

Maybe Carmen saw the uncertain looks on the faces around her. So she explained. "But he's fun too. He makes *enchiladas* and refried beans to die for. We got Mexican pizza, and my cousin sings and Mama dances. She's hot. Mama goes crazy when we have a party. She's worse than the kids. She is totally *loca*. You're coming, right Ernie?"

Carmen's invitation left Ernesto in a state of shock. He wasn't quite sure what he was in for, but he nodded yes. "I'll be there, Carmen."

"Everybody who comes to my parties is good," Carmen asserted. "No creeps allowed. Like Clay Aguirre can't come. No gang wannabes or potheads or dopers of any kind."

Even Julio's father, who had seen much of the world—much of it bad—began to laugh.

That Saturday night, Ernesto made his way to Nuthatch Lane. He immediately picked out Carmen's house because it was the only hot pink house on the street. When Ernesto came into the house, about ten kids from Chavez High were already there. He saw Julio, Eddie, and Jorge, and then Abel Ruiz came in. There were also some girls Ernesto didn't know. One boy held a guitar in his arms, and he wore a big sombrero. Ernesto assumed he was the singing cousin. Beside him was a beautiful girl in a red dress. She didn't look like she was in high school. She looked older, and she wore a lot of makeup.

"There's my cousin, Oscar Perez," Carmen explained. "He's gonna sing now. He sings *magnífico, espléndido!* Conchita is going to sing too, and dance. She's a wonderful dancer."

The lady in the red dress spun around as Oscar wailed out Mexican ballads of love and betrayal. By now, about twenty-five guests had showed up, and everybody was clapping and cheering.

Ernesto noticed a big, burly man with a mustache standing at the side of the room. He looked like he might be Emilio Zapata Ibarra because he wore a plastic star on his black shirt and his arms were folded belligerently. His dark eyes darted about the room, looking for trouble.

"Oscar is good, huh?" Carmen asked, nudging Ernesto.

"Yeah, and that lady. She's amazing," Ernesto remarked.

"Mama is a wonderful dancer," Carmen agreed. "She danced in a group when she was a teenager, and now she's a *salsera*. She gives dance lessons."

"Your mama?" Ernesto gasped. "*That* lady is . . . your mama?"

"Yeah," Carmen giggled. "Oscar is in a band now too, and they sound awesome. They are like Ozomatli and Quetzal Guerrero. Oscar's going places."

Carmen's mother tied an apron over her red dress and brought in the Mexican pizza, hot from the oven. "Mom can do everything," Carmen proclaimed. "She is thirty-five years old, and, when people meet her, they think she's twenty-five. We got good genes in our family."

"Wow!" Ernesto cried, munching on a slice of pie. "This is great pizza!"

"Yeah," Carmen agreed. "It's got tomato and chilies and shredded, taco-flavored cheese." Then the girl paused. "Uh-oh. Here comes Papa. He knows everybody else here, but you're a stranger to him. He will be wanting to know all about you. Don't be nervous, Ernie. He looks fierce, but he is really a nice man."

The mustachioed man drew closer to Ernesto and inquired, "So you are—?"

"Ernesto Sandoval," Ernesto replied in a voice that suddenly went up an octave and sounded like a hinge needing oil. "My father teaches history at Cesar Chavez High School. His name is Luis Sandoval."

"He's such a good teacher too," Carmen chimed in. "All the kids like him because he's smart and interesting and very fair. We all love him—except for the losers, you know, the dregs of humanity who sit way in the back and try to make trouble. But who cares about them?"

"Ah," Mr. Ibarra said with a smile, "your father is a teacher. Very good. I admire educated men. I admire teachers and doctors and priests, but they must be men who have compassion. *Simpático*. I have no use for arrogant men who use their education to lord it over others."

"My father has a lot of compassion," Ernesto responded, still nervously.

Just then Ernesto spotted two guys he did not expect to see at the party. They arrived late. Dom Reynosa and Carlos Negrete had come strolling in, uninvited, because they heard the music and they wanted to join the party. Ernesto shuddered. Dom and Carlos were the guys eager to drop out of Cesar Chavez High School, the ones tagging every fence and bare wall in the *barrio*. But Ernesto saw a silver lining in their arrival. They were just the guys to explain to Mr. Ibarra how much compassion his father had.

"Hey Carlos! . . . Dom!" Ernesto called to them. "Come on over here and have some pizza. I was telling Carmen's father about my dad and how compassionate he is at school." Ernesto hoped Carlos and Dom could talk about his father rescuing them from the wrong road they were taking by getting them to do a school mural. "Tell Mr. Ibarra about the great mural you guys are doing . . ."

But Emilio Zapata Ibarra did not seem too happy to see the boys in his home. He gave them such a withering look that both boys' heads seemed to retreat into their shirt collars, making them shorter. "I think these are the dregs of humanity that Carmen was talking about," he growled. "I have nabbed these two myself while they painted ugly graffiti on the side of the fence at the corner." He turned to his daughter. "Carmen, did you invite them here?"

"No Papa," Carmen answered shrewdly, "but they are not very bad boys. Dom's mother goes to Our Lady of Guadalupe Church every morning and lights candles for her children, especially for Dom."

Carlos spoke up quickly. He knew Mr. Ibarra, an extremely large and mean-looking man. One time, when he and Dom were tagging, Mr. Ibarra lifted Carlos up into the air by his coat. "Uh sir, we were doing bad in school," Carlos started to explain. "But Mr. Sandoval, he uh . . . kinda changed everything. He could see we uh . . . weren't doing so good. So he wanted to give us something to do that we'd like so we'd, you know, stay in school, you know. And now, you know, we're doing this mural and, you know . . ."

"Stop saying 'you know,'" Mr. Ibarra demanded in his booming voice. "Of course, I know. Do I look like an *idiota?*"

"Oh no, sir," Dom replied, fearful that Carlos' stumbling explanation would cause them to be thrown out. "No, no, you seem like a smart guy. Real smart." Dom wanted to appease the frightening-looking mustachioed man.

"Anyway," Carlos hurried on, anxious to make his case before all vestiges of friendliness left Mr. Ibarra's face. "Mr. Sandoval took us under his wing, and now we're gonna stay in school and really try to do better." He stopped himself from saying "you know" in the nick of time. "We're gonna paint this great mural and other stuff too."

"We're all done with tagging," Dom affirmed. "No more of that, no sirree. Mr. Sandoval said we can't be doing that because we're gonna be artists like that José Orozco and . . . the other guy . . ."

"Diego Rivera," Carlos supplied the name.

"Yeah, that's the dude," Dom agreed.

"See," Ernesto chimed in, "my father really cares about the kids in his classes. When he sees students who look like they might be dropping out, he tries to give them a reason to stay. I'm really proud of my father, Mr. Ibarra."

Mr. Ibarra seemed impressed. He smiled warmly at Ernesto. "I like a son who is proud of his father," he said warmly. "That is an excellent quality in a young man." He glanced at Carmen and remarked, "This is a fine young man you invited here." Then he looked at Dom and Carlos, and he commanded, "You *muchachos* have some pizza now. Pizza and soda and *aguas frescas*. No liquor here. Not in my house."

Dom and Carlos scrambled toward the food, moving quickly as if they'd just made a narrow escape.

Oscar Perez started singing again, lightening up the atmosphere. This time he performed Mexican and Central American songs. He threw in some Latin rock and reggae, which all the kids enjoyed. Mrs. Ibarra stripped off her apron and began to dance, and everybody else joined in. A big smile broke on Mr. Ibarra's face, and he clapped his hands merrily as the room filled with music and the swirling colors of the dancers' clothes.

Ernesto found Carmen in his arms, and he held her close as they danced. Then, holding her hand, he spun her around. For just a few minutes, Ernesto was so taken with the beauty and sweetness of the girl that he forgot Naomi Martinez. Carmen giggled happily, her brown eyes dancing and filling with light.

When the evening ended, Ernesto thanked Mr. and Mrs. Ibarra for the wonderful evening, and he thanked Carmen for inviting him. Ernesto made special mention of how good the food was. "You are a wonderful cook, Mrs. Ibarra," he said, "and your dancing was very beautiful."

"I like this *muchacho,* Carmen," Mrs. Ibarra laughed. "You must bring him here often."

As Ernesto walked toward the door, he realized he was being followed. A very large shadow fell across his back. He turned to see Emilio Zapata Iabarra close behind him. The man grasped Ernesto by the shoulder and told him, "I like you very much, Ernesto Sandoval. You are a fine young man, and I am very impressed with you."

"Uh, thank you, sir," Ernesto replied.

"You are also," Mr. Ibarra went on in a deep soulful voice, "the son of an eminent teacher. You have the compassion to reach out to those two bad boys. You lead them from their wicked ways of tagging and ruining the looks of the *barrio*. I salute this man—your father!"

Ernesto was getting more nervous by the minute. Mr. Ibarra's speechmaking seemed very much over the top. Ernesto looked out longingly into the darkness. He wished he were already hurrying down the walk on his way home.

"I just want you to know, Ernesto," Mr. Ibarra continued, "that it is all right with me that you are good friends with my daughter. I approve of this. I love her dearly, and I want only the best for her. And you are one of the best. I can see that. I know my daughter is not perfect, but she has a very good heart, and she has inherited her mother's beauty. As you can see, I have a rather large nose, and I was fearful my daughter could inherit that, but she did not."

Mr. Ibarra laughed happily at his observation. Ernesto continued peering into the darkness, wishing he were out there, on his way home.

"Unfortunately," Mr. Ibarra persisted, "Carmen has one big fault. She never stops talking. But you can say *silencio* in a very firm voice, and usually she will stop. Although sometimes I must go outside and sit in the car until she is quiet. But that is a small fault in so lovely a girl."

Ernesto didn't know quite what to make of Mr. Ibarra. The man was acting as if Ernesto and Carmen had just become engaged. What did he think? "Uh, well, Carmen and I are good *school* friends, and I like her. She's really nice. I mean, she's a great *school* friend, you know . . ." Ernesto usually did not sprinkle his conversation with "You-know's," but he was extremely nervous.

Finally the man's large hand released Ernesto's shoulder, and he smiled warmly, his mustache twitching in a strange way. He seemed very happy.

"Goodnight sir," Ernesto bid farewell gratefully, sprinting down the walk to the street.

Ernesto glanced up at the moon. Venus was nearby. He had only a couple blocks to get home. But it was almost eleven o'clock, and the sky was dark, even with a few street lights shining. Ernesto couldn't help wondering who else was out tonight. Nor could he help thinking about Tommy Alvarado and how he'd been alive this time last week. Tommy had been dating Yvette then. His biggest problems were getting good grades in history and math and maybe doing his job in the parking lot.

Ernesto wondered whether Tommy had any idea how dangerous it was to be dating Coyote's girl. Did he ever give it a thought that being with Yvette could cost him his life? Then Ernesto thought about Naomi Martinez and how he had tried to get closer to her. But that situation was different, wasn't it? Clay wasn't a gangbanger like Coyote. He was just a garden-variety jerk.

Or could you really know about such things before it was too late?

CHAPTER NINE

Ernesto hurried down the street, not paying much attention to the voices of other people he heard. A man on the porch across the street was cursing someone. Two men walked down the street, hauling garbage bags containing their life possessions. Ernesto felt sorry for them. A woman passed, pushing a shopping cart with her stuff in it. Ernesto was too embarrassed even to look at her. Seeing homeless men was bad enough, but homeless women really got to him. Somebody's mother? Somebody's grandmother?

"Got change?" a female voice, made raspy by cigarette smoke, asked from behind Ernesto.

He turned. She had white hair, but she didn't seem that old. She was missing a lot of teeth. Her hands trembled when she reached out for Ernesto's change. He gave her two dollars, and her eyes lit up. She'd expected a couple quarters. "*Gracias!*" she said. She didn't look Mexican, but she could see the boy was by his dark skin. She hurried now, pushing her shopping cart toward the little all-night store at the end of the street. She could get a sixteen-ounce cup of coffee and two hot dogs. It was maybe the best thing that happened to her all day.

Ernesto turned away from the woman and walked off in the dark. Ernesto remembered something that his Grandma Vasquez had told him. In Los Angeles, the Vasquezes lived in a better neighborhood than this. Ernesto and his family used to live in that neighborhood too, when Dad taught school up there. Mom's parents were sad and worried when Ernesto and his family moved away. They did not want their daughter, Maria Vasquez Sandoval, to move to the *barrio* where she had been born.

"We put that bad neighborhood behind us," Ernesto's grandmother lamented, "and have a better life here."

"But Mama," Ernesto's mother had protested, "Luis was laid off from the school here. Cesar Chavez High School wants to hire him. We have no choice."

CHAPTER NINE

Ernesto's mother's parents were younger than Dad's parents. They were still in their fifties, and both were working. Dad's father was already dead, and *Abuela* Lena was in her seventies. Ernesto had always felt closer to his father's parents because Mom's parents seemed to love money and success too much. Ernesto had nothing against money and success, and he wanted both. But they seemed almost obsessed with getting ahead.

"The dropout rate at that school where your father will teach is seventeen percent," Mom's mother moaned. "That is the school you will be going to, Ernie. Katalina and Juanita too, eventually. It just seems like the whole family is going backward instead of forward."

"We'll be fine, Grandma," Ernesto had said, assuringly.

"Ernie," Grandma Vasquez said in an almost fierce voice. "You must finish high school and go to college. We wanted that for Maria. We were crushed when she didn't go to college. But you must. Do you hear me? *You must go to college, Ernie!*"

Now Ernesto knew what *Abuela* meant by her words. She didn't want her grandson to have to put with beggars on the street.

He also remembered something his dad had said long ago. "You can't fix everything, but you can make little differences by being kind." Luis Sandoval had told his son this when he was just a small boy. His words showed how the man felt about such "beggars."

Ernesto Sandoval never doubted that he would graduate from high school and go on to college. He wanted a good career, something fulfilling. Luis Sandoval loved teaching; teaching defined him. Ernesto could not imagine his father as anything but a teacher. Ernesto wanted something like that, something he loved and was good at.

CHAPTER TEN

On Sunday afternoon, Ernesto checked on the computer and found that the 1992 Volvo was still available for five hundred dollars. Ernesto had saved four hundred dollars from birthday and Christmas gifts. Now he added another hundred from working at the pizzeria. Ernesto's father drove him to the small used car lot so that he could look at the car. He knew his friends, and especially Clay Aguirre and his gang, would laugh at him if he bought the Volvo. But he needed a reliable car for the time being. The ad said the car worked well, and Ernesto liked that. He didn't have money for costly repairs.

"There's the place, Ernie," Dad noted, slowing down. About fifteen cars were on the lot, all of them old. The lot was not high end. It was a place where poor people and kids came looking for the cheapest wheels they could find. When Ernesto got out of the minivan, he spotted the Volvo right away. It was big and ugly. He winced. What was he thinking? He glanced at some of the other cars—a cool looking Honda Accord and a Toyota pickup, bright red and cute. Ernesto had second thoughts about the Volvo.

Ernesto's father stayed back, hanging around the minivan. This was Ernesto's deal. He wasn't going to give advice. He would get involved only if Ernesto asked him to.

"How much is the Honda?" Ernesto asked the salesperson, liking the sharp metallic blue color.

"A thousand dollars," the dealer responded. He looked Middle Eastern. A lot of used car lots and small stores in the *barrio* were run by guys from Iraq and from the emirates around the Gulf. Like the

Mexican Americans, the Asians, and the African Americans in the neighborhood, they didn't have much money.

A thousand dollars? Ernesto thought about the five hundred in his wallet. He wasn't going to sign up for car payments. He couldn't afford them. No way.

"How much is the Toyota pickup?" he asked hopefully. He could imagine driving that little truck. Naomi in the cab with him. The vision came to him even though he'd promised himself not to fantasize about her. The thought made him smile.

"Eight fifty," the dealer said.

Even standing where he was, leaning on the side door of the minivan, Luis Sandoval could see the disappointment on his son's face. Ernesto wanted the red pickup. The desire was all over his face. Dad came walking over. He said to Ernesto, "Ernie, I could lend you a couple hundred, and you could pay me back when you're able. I mean, if you want the pickup."

Ernesto shook his head. "Thanks Dad, but no. I would be less than a man if I didn't pay for my own car."

He walked grimly to the Volvo. It really wasn't a bad looking car. It just wasn't the kind of car a sixteen-year-old kid wanted to drive.

"Is it reliable?" he asked the dealer.

"You bet," the dealer assured him. "It belonged to a lady who bought it new. She took good care of it. Now her son had to put her in a nursing home. You know how it goes." A smile slashed the dealer's face. "Nice finish. Clean engine."

"It said online it was five hundred," Ernesto said.

"Yep," the dealer affirmed.

"Okay then," Ernesto said. "Can I take a look at the engine? How about a test drive?"

"Sure," the dealer said, opening the hood. "Let me see your driver's license, and we'll fill out a little paperwork. The engine's a beauty."

After peering at the engine and driving the car a few blocks, Ernesto was satisfied. He followed the dealer into the small prefab office and signed some papers for transfer of ownership. He gave the man his five hundred dollars and came out with the keys.

Luis Sandoval smiled at his son. "I guess you'll be driving it home," he suggested. "Congratulations, *mi hijo*. I didn't get my first car until I was twenty."

Ernesto slid behind the wheel. He didn't want *this* car, but he wanted any car so badly that he felt happy. He was excited to think that, when he needed to go somewhere, he could just go and not ask his parents for a ride. The Volvo would be waiting for him in the driveway like a patient horse.

The engine roared to life, and Ernesto was in motion. He grinned in spite of himself. Driving his own car felt so good. Even though it was a big, old, white Volvo, he caught sight of himself in the rearview mirror, grinning.

When Ernesto pulled into the driveway, Mom came out with the girls. Juanita cried, "It's a pretty car! I like it!" Katalina, though she was only eight and too wise for her age, commented, "It's not very cool."

"Thanks Kat," Ernesto replied, grimacing. "I needed that."

"It's a nice, safe car," Mom stated, making matters worse. "That's what counts. Who cares what it looks like?"

Ernesto went into the house and texted Abel. "Got the car. Ugly Volvo."

Then he texted Gabriella. "Got a cool new car. U should C it. Wish U could ride in it."

On Monday morning, Ernesto took the car to school, parking it in the lot at Cesar Chavez High School. As luck would have it, Naomi Martinez was just arriving with Aguirre. Clay drove a used but way cooler Mustang. Clay hurried over to the Volvo, foiling Ernesto's plans to escape from the car before anybody saw him getting out of it.

"Hey stick boy, did you steal your grandma's car?" Clay yelled. He began to laugh hysterically. Naomi gave him a poke and told him to stop laughing, but she just made him all the louder and nastier. Whenever Naomi displayed the least bit of feeling for anyone, Clay really poured it on. "Ain't your grandma gonna be mad that you stole her car? Old folks love their Volvos. What did you want to do something like that for?"

Some of Clay's friends appeared to join in the fun.

"You ain't never gonna ask a chick to ride in that thing, are you?" a tall boy yelled.

"She'd have to wear a lampshade over her head," another guy added.

Ernesto felt his face turning warm. He read once about how hound dogs treed raccoons in the South. The poor raccoon would be stuck up the tree, and the dogs were leaping at the trunk of the tree and howling. The raccoon had no way to escape.

Ernesto felt like a treed raccoon. He knew he'd catch some razzing about the Volvo, but he didn't expect this kind of attention. The crowd grew. The jeers got louder. The whole football team was joining in.

Ernesto glanced at Naomi. Her face showed pain. She hated what was happening, but she didn't do anything. She didn't have the courage to tell Clay to stop. Ernesto felt anger for her, but then he remembered how her father treated her mother. She had to just stand there and take it. She was well taught. You sucked it up. The thought made Ernesto sick.

Suddenly somebody was behind Ernesto, somebody who'd come walking up, attracted by the commotion in the parking lot. Abel Ruiz came up alongside Ernesto, his arms folded over his chest. "So you got wheels, Ernie," he commented in a dogged voice. "Way to go."

"He got a granny car," Clay howled.

"I got no car at all," Abel retorted. "I wouldn't mind driving it myself."

Then Eddie Gonzales and Jorge Aguilar, from the track team, showed up. They stood alongside Ernesto, and Eddie yelled at Clay Aguirre. "Hey man, you got nothing better to do than stand around making a fool of yourself? Why don't you go study? We got a test coming up in English. You better do good, or you won't be wearing no football jersey no more."

"Yeah Clay," Jorge added. "When you get kicked off the team for being a *bobo,* you'll be public enemy number one around here. The team depends on you man."

Ernesto was surprised and then awe-struck. Others kept coming. Julio Avila arrived. He walked up to the Volvo and commented, "Good car, Sandoval. My brother got one, and it ran for three hundred thousand miles. I might get me one."

Four guys were standing with Ernesto when Dom and Carlos showed up.

"We got your back, homeboy," Dom whispered to Ernesto.

"Your old man went to bat for us, and we're going to bat for you, homie," Carlos added.

Pretty soon the guys standing with Ernesto outnumbered Clay Aguirre's crowd, which was getting smaller and smaller. Clay turned and snarled, "I got no time to be standing here talking trash with a bunch of losers." He grabbed Naomi's hand and took off toward the school.

Ernesto turned and smiled at the other boys. "Thanks!" he said.

"Anytime, man," Abel Ruiz assured him, speaking for them all.

When he got home from work that night, Ernesto told his mother how six friends had stood up for him this morning when Clay Aguirre was giving him a hard time about the Volvo. "A couple weeks ago I was a stranger," he mused. "And now all these guys turn up. Mom, it was amazing."

Ernesto's mother smiled. "Most of the kids in the *barrio* are great," she advised him. "It was the same when I was growing up here. I had good friends who I could turn to whenever I needed help. You know, I left here ten years ago, but I'm reconnecting with good friends, and it's wonderful. I miss my parents up in LA, but it's good to be home where I grew up and went to school. Oh Ernie, I knew you'd fit in fine. I know you were worried in the beginning, but you're such a neat kid. I knew friends would come like bees to honey."

"Mom, this girl Naomi. I've told you about her," Ernesto confided.

"Yes, Linda and Felix's daughter," Mom responded, looking troubled.

"All the time Clay Aguirre, her boyfriend, was on my case about the Volvo," Ernesto continued, "she looked so hurt. I could see she hated what he was doing, but she just stood there. Why does she want to be with a guy like that? I don't get it, Mom." But Ernesto did sort of did get it.

"I knew Linda—Naomi's mom—when I was a kid," Mom explained. "She was older than me when we were growing up, but we were friends, sorta. It's a culture for some people, honey. A girl wanting a strong, tough guy and expecting to follow his lead. I remember when Linda was dating Felix. Just seeing them together made me shudder because he was mean and sarcastic, always putting her down. But you couldn't talk to her and make her see that."

Mom shook her head. "I remember when I met your father. There he was, this tall, skinny guy with glasses. A nerd, but cute, really cute. My heart started pounding. I admired him because he was soft-spoken, a real gentleman. He respected me, Ernie. He had a graciousness about him, still does. I never got to go to college, and I knew that was a disappointment to my parents. But, you know, I just knew that marrying him was the right thing for us. Now, when anything comes up, your father asks me what I think, and *he really cares*. It touches me so deeply that we're really partners. I feel so blessed to have him. I feel sorry for women like Linda and Naomi who get put down and just hang their heads and suffer."

"Mom," Ernesto commented, "Naomi is pretty and smart. And one time in class she had done a report for Aguirre, and she forgot to bring it in. He yelled at her in front of everybody, called her all kinds of ugly names. I mean, he made me so mad. Somebody needs to set her straight."

"Sweetheart," Mom replied, "don't fall in love with the girl you wish she was. Don't ever do that. She is who she is. Kids make that mistake. Older people make it too. They fall in love with somebody who's all wrong, but they have this ideal version of the person in their mind. They think, by magic, this is the person they are going to end up with."

Ernesto looked away. He knew Mom was making sense, but he didn't want to hear it.

He looked out the window, where Katalina and Juanita were playing. They were jumping rope. Katalina was being bossy as usual. Juanita was fighting back. Juanita was no wimp. They played tug-of-war with the jump rope for a while, each wanting it for herself. Then they were friends again. They were just little kids. They'd change as they grew. Katalina would not be so bossy.

"Mom," Ernesto remarked, "Naomi is only sixteen. She could change. She doesn't have to go down the same road her mom went."

"Just be careful, Ernie," Mom advised. "I don't want you getting hurt. I don't want you chasing a mirage."

"I know, Mom," Ernesto said.

He got up and went to his room to work on his computer. He had to finish the science report for Mr. Escalante's class. He sat there for a few minutes, staring at the computer screen.

He was trying to focus, but he kept thinking about Naomi. She looked so intense when she was answering a question in class. He loved to watch her. She twirled her pen in her graceful little hand when she was pondering something. That was so cute. He thought about how she cocked her pretty head and then tossed it to get the curls out of her face and off her amazingly smooth cheek. Ernesto thought about how Naomi looked in those bright sweaters and tops that she liked to wear. He remembered how happy he was on the day she wanted to hang with him and they went to Hortencia's. For a little while, Ernesto thought that he was going to get his wish, that they were getting close, and that maybe he had a chance. Then she made up with Clay Aguirre.

Ernesto got up from the computer chair and walked over to his bookcase. He took down last year's yearbook. He flipped through the pages again to look at her picture, taken when she was a sophomore. The seniors had large, nice photographs, but the sophomores had only small pictures. Still, Naomi was a cheerleader. So there were other pictures of her—cute pictures of Naomi and the other cheerleaders in their black and red outfits. She looked so good. That big smile and those eyes just melted his heart. He stared at one picture of her atop a pyramid of cheerleaders, holding her pom-poms aloft. She was so beautiful.

Ernesto flipped some more pages, looking for more pictures of her. But another face caught his eye. It was that of a freshman girl. She wasn't beautiful like Naomi Martinez, but she was pretty. She had large, soulful eyes and long, straight hair. She seemed to be looking out on the world and uttering a silent plea: "Don't hurt me, world. I'm struggling. I've always been struggling. I haven't found my place yet, and I'm scared. Don't hurt me. I'll try to be whatever you want me to be. I'm not very strong or smart or stuff like that. I'm more scared than anything. Just don't hurt me, please."

The face of the girl was so compelling that Ernesto checked out her name. He wondered whether she'd come back to Chavez High this year and whether she was a sophomore now? The names were at the bottom of the page, reading left to right. Hers was in the middle.

The name startled Ernesto, jolted him. He hadn't recognized Yvette Ozono—the girl at Tommy Alvarado's funeral. Coyote's victim. The girl who was crying over the casket of the boy who tried and failed to save her, the boy she loved well but too late.

A wave of deep sadness engulfed Ernesto like a powerful ocean tide.

But he stubbornly would not give up his dream of winning Naomi's heart. She had to finally understand that Clay Aguirre was all wrong for her. She was a smart girl. She just had to get real. There had to be a way for Ernesto to help her understand that she was better than Clay, that she wasn't doomed to repeat her mother's experience. Then maybe Ernesto would have a chance with her. Maybe she would ride in his ugly old white Volvo for the time being. And later, maybe she would join him in the cool car he would eventually get. He was not going to let go of the hope in his heart.

"Ernie," he thought to himself, "you have some friends now. You're running track. And a lot of the students and teachers at Chavez know you. You have a job, and you have a car. Most important, you may have a shot at hooking up with the greatest girl in the school. You don't have to feel like a complete stranger anymore."